you are not ~~LAZY~~

LET'S CHAT WITH SUCCESS

You Are Not Lazy
By Sirshree Tejparkhi

Copyright © Tejgyan Global Foundation
All Rights Reserved 2015

Tejgyan Global Foundation is a charitable organization with its headquarters in Pune, India

ISBN : 978-81-8415-413-9

Published by WOW Publishings Pvt. Ltd., India

First edition published in August 2015

Second edition published in April 2017

Second reprint in December 2022

Printed and bound by Trinity Academy, Pune, INDIA

Copyright and publishing rights are vested exclusively with WOW Publishings Pvt. Ltd. This book is sold subject to the condition that it shall not by way of trade or otherwise, be lent, resold, hired out, or otherwise circulated without the publisher's prior written consent in any form of binding or cover other than that in which it is published and without a similar condition including this condition being imposed on the subsequent purchaser and without limiting the rights under copyright reserved above, no part of this publication may be reproduced, stored in or introduced into a retrieval system, or transmitted, in any form, or by any means, electronic, mechanical, photocopying, recording or otherwise, without the prior written permission of both the copyright owner and the above-mentioned publisher of this book. Any person who does any unauthorized act in relation to this publication may be liable to criminal prosecution and civil claims for damages.

Although the author and publisher have made every effort to ensure accuracy of content in this book, they hereby disclaim any liability to any party for any loss, damage, or disruption caused by errors or omissions, resulting from negligence, accident, or any other cause. Readers are advised to take full responsibility to exercise discretion in understanding and applying the content of this book.

This book is dedicated to

THOMAS EDISON

who never shirked work nor
made excuses for work which
could not be completed
By inventing the light bulb
he brightened the world
which made it possible for
many other inventions to
take place

THE THREAD OF CONVERSATIONS

LET'S CHAT WITH SUCCESS — 7

CONVERSATION 1
You cannot be lazy!
Know some interesting stuff about the body. — 24

CONVERSATION 2
Let's peep into a lazy person's lifestyle
and have some fun. — 42

CONVERSATION 3
Is lethargy **that** dangerous? — 53

CONVERSATION 4
Of course, you'd never want **these**
habits to lead you to failure! — 63

CONVERSATION 5
Who knew you could be even mentally lazy! — 71

CONVERSATION 6
Rest is important...
but there's a right way to rest and a wrong way too! — 81

CONVERSATION 7
It's okay to sleep a little longer...
if you don't want an awesome life! — 93

CONVERSATION 8
What if you were completely drained?
You'd be asleep, or dead! — 105

CONVERSATION 9
Diving into the pool of excuses?
...Ask 1 question and 10 solutions will pour in. — 115

CONVERSATION 10
Who does boring tasks?
The one who doesn't find it boring! — 126

CONVERSATION 11
What is your highest choice for this life
as well as for the afterlife? — 140

CONVERSATION 12
Stasis due to stress.
He did taste success once... later success eluded him. — 152

CONVERSATION 13
"Who am I?"
A bomb for the lethargic individual! — 164

CONVERSATION 14
My body... HIS temple! — 176

CONVERSATION 15
Ask nature and it will liberate you from lethargy. — 185

YOU ARE DESTINED TO SUCCEED! — 191

APPENDIX
FAQs on Lethargy
About Tej Gyan Foundation — 198–216

Let's Chat with Success

The alarm went off and Ankit sank deeper into his blanket. But the alarm continued relentlessly. Ankit desperately wanted that shrill sound to stop, but didn't feel like moving a muscle. Thankfully, the sound stopped after a few seconds, and feeling better, he drifted back to sleep.

After two minutes, the alarm dutifully started again. "That's it! I'm going to crush all the alarms of the world!" Feeling irritated enough to pull his hand out, he shut the alarm with a loud thud.

"ANKIT, wake up! Rohit has already left for school. It's high time, you have to get up now or you'll be late for college again..." His mother's words fell on deaf ears.

"Lazy Prince! What sort of example are you setting for your younger brother? And do you remember today you'd be getting the result for the job placement? Are you going to get through at least this time? Third time lucky? Or are you planning to spend your whole life sleeping and eating with your father's earnings?" The caustic words of his dad reached his ears.

"Oh, no! Results today!"

He got ready in a jiffy, stuffing a paratha in his mouth and grabbing another one, ran out looking totally disheveled, with his mother calling out from behind. He drove at a dangerously high speed, yet reached his college late—as usual. Parking his bike, combing back his hair with his fingers, he rushed towards the Placement Coordinator's Office. There was a crowd at the notice board.

"What's the hurry, dude? You're not going anywhere." His friend Vihaan called out. Hearing this, his heartbeat climbed further. But he decided to ignore his friend. Pushing through the crowd, with his heart thudding in his chest, he searched for his name. He couldn't believe it. He looked again with blurry eyes. No. No Ankit Vaidya. But sure enough, Vihaan Sabarwal was second on the list. His heart sank.

"Relax, bro. You can at least feel happy for me!" Vihaan came up to him.

"Sure… congrats, man!" mumbled Ankit, trying hard to recover.

"Give me double congrats! You can't imagine how happy I am! Late last night I got an email confirming my admission in Harvard Business School. Can you imagine? HARVARD."

"Oh, really? That's great! Congrats once again… But that means you're not going to take this job?"

"Who needs this job?! I have bigger plans."

"I know…I know."

"It's party time! My parents are giving a party at our house today. And of course, you are invited."

"Oh, sure."

"I heard the word PARTY. Who's giving a party?" Their friend Tanisha joined in.

"Hey, Tanisha, good you came! I'm giving a party for my admission in Harvard plus this job offer."

"What?! That's totally crazy!"

"I know, right? You are coming to the party today evening at my home."

"I'd love that! And what about you, Ankit? Did you get a placement too?"

Ankit wanted to disappear in the ground, but tried to act casual. "Forget it *yaar*! That company isn't good enough for me. It's too small and insignificant. I'd also like to go abroad for further studies and become a big businessman… only if my father supported me."

"Yeah, right. Wouldn't we all? Hey, listen, I'd love to sit and chat, but I got to run. See you guys later, bye."

"Bye."

That evening Ankit returned home with a feeling of dread. He had ignored his father's calls earlier in the day, but couldn't avoid him at home.

***

After the verbal and emotional onslaught of his parents as well as the smirks and wise cracks of his brother, Ankit was in no mood to attend Vihaan's party. But unfortunately Vihaan's dad had invited his family too. Bad situation. Just as he started to say something, his dad stopped him dead. "Stop making excuses for everything! And you're always going for parties, then what's the problem with this one? Are you feeling embarrassed that Vihaan succeeded and you did not? Maybe this embarrassment will push you to do something. Or if you had paid attention, you could have learnt a thing or two from that boy. Anyway, YOU ARE COMING. That's final."

The party was at the terrace of Vihaan's house. Everybody was laughing and enjoying. Vihaan's parents were beaming. Ankit's father patted Vihaan's back and congratulated him. Rohit immediately darted off to find someone his own age. Vihaan smiled happily and mingled around. Ankit too was sporting a smile, but felt hollow inside.

His father congratulated Vihaan's dad. "You must be really proud of your son, Mr. Sabarwal. He's a fine young man with a bright future. I wish my son Ankit too could be at least a bit like him. To tell you the truth, I'm worried about his future. He's so lazy, I'm not even sure if he'll pass the final exams…"

Ankit was stunned. It felt like he had been punched in the gut and his breath was knocked out of his chest. His fake smile faded. He couldn't believe his father had said that… openly… in front of everyone. He literally wanted to be the Hollow Man right now. He scrambled away from the scene in a daze, filled with embarrassment and hurt.

He desperately needed a change in mood. He looked around for his friends. But he found them all clustered around Vihaan. Unwillingly he joined the group but soon regretted it. Not just because everybody was either talking to Vihaan or talking about Vihaan, but also because hardly anybody noticed him or spoke to him. Feeling ignored, he slipped away to get some snacks.

At the snacks counter, he came across Vihaan's aunt. "Hi, Ankit. Did you get a placement too? No?! Then what are you going to do now?" This question cut him to the quick. He didn't know what to say. He simply couldn't take it anymore. He walked off the terrace and escaped to Vihaan's room. Here no one would bother him—hopefully.

Sipping a cold drink, he looked around. There were lots of books in the room, then there were various posters, and then his eye fell upon the shelf of trophies! There were trophies and awards of all sizes and shapes that Vihaan had received since his childhood. This sight added salt to his wounds. Each one reminded him how Vihaan had won and he had failed. He approached the shelf and took the shiniest trophy in his hand. He wondered why some people could easily achieve success and he could not. He felt like smashing it there and then. But controlled himself.

He gave a piercing look to the trophy once again. "I WANT YOU, NO MATTER WHAT. YOU HAVE TO COME TO ME." Saying so, he put it inside his jacket and left.

He drove back alone to his house. Entering his room he pushed off some of the mess on his table and plunked the trophy. He stared intently at it. "Why have you always eluded me? WHY?" Feeling agitated, he started pacing the room, thinking how he could change his condition. He knew he should work harder and put in more effort in his studies, but he just couldn't bring himself to do it. His body-mind had got so habituated to his comfort zone, that it was extremely difficult to get out of it. He didn't know what to do. He could not think of anybody who could help him. His pacing became even more intense. He felt as if he was going crazy. "I WANT SUCCESS. I NEED SUCCESS NOW. Is there nobody in the world who can help me?" He screamed.

"There is. I can help you," said a soft voice.

Ankit was startled. He stopped and looked around. No one. He glanced outside his window. Still, no one. He opened his door and peeped out. His family had not yet returned from the party. He went out and checked the entire perimeter of his house. No one again. He came back and checked all his gadgets. Nothing.

"It's me—Success. You want me, don't you?"

"Who's this? TELL ME NOW. I'm definitely not in the mood for any jokes!"

"Nor am I. I sincerely wish to help you." The voice seemed to come from the... *trophy*.

Ankit picked up the trophy and scrutinized it from every aspect. But it had no electronic devices attached to it.

"I can be a trophy for some people. I can be name and fame for some others. I can be a particular job position or status for some. I can be a bungalow and car for somebody. I can be a happy family for some. While for some I can be a new invention. For some I can be the discovery of something for the upliftment of mankind. Some want me in the materialistic plane and some in the spiritual plane. It depends on each individual's understanding and level of consciousness."

"So, you are…"

"I am Success. You called for me, and here I am."

"Whoa! I must have truly lost my mind. I hope I haven't developed schizophrenia or something… I am hearing VOICES!"

"Don't worry, you haven't lost it! 😊 In fact I will help you find all that you have lost and all that you can find in this life."

"How can I believe you? Maybe somebody is playing a trick on me."

"I thought you wanted to stop playing and attain me seriously."

"I do, but…"

"Just cool down and listen, dear. You have nothing to lose and much to gain."

"Ok, fine. I will listen. This is my last year in college and I want to score well in my exams and then have a great career. So, tell me, how can you help me with that?"

"I will tell you how to attain success if you are seriously ready to listen. So, are you?"

Ankit took a deep breath. "Yes, I need success and I am ready to listen. Tell me."

"OK. First of all, sit down calmly. Secondly, broaden your mind because there are certain things I'll tell you which you may not initially believe, but they are the reality. Listen with an open mind and you shall receive the best and the highest."

"OK. Terms and conditions accepted."

"Great, then let's begin. I know how much you yearn for me. But you have no idea that I'm more eager to be a part of your life than you could have ever been."

"Really?! Well, that feels good... But you never showed up."

"That's because your eyes have always been filled with dreams of success but your journey has never taken off from the planning stage. You know you are full of potential, and success was and still is just around the corner. I see you dreaming big and formulating strategies. So, even I fasten my seatbelt happily to enjoy the ride with you. But I can't be with you unless you make it happen. You tend to get distracted. You're always indulging in something irrelevant when it's time for you to take action. Please don't mind, but I guess I need to take over the wheel and drive, for now at least, later on you can take over. This is because success means doing what you decide.

Remember, everyone has the potential to do what one wants to do. It's really very simple: Decide, Plan and Do."

"That's it?! Is the formula of success that simple?"

"Yes, it is. You can easily attain me if you follow this simple but powerful formula. Ok, tell me what type of success do you want?"

"What do you mean by what type?"

"Well, as I've mentioned before, success is different things for different people. But broadly, there are three types of success:

First type is success as per your own understanding. This kind of success is that in which you achieve what you have determined to and accomplish it as per your planned method. For example, you want to be an actor or writer or dancer or anything else, and you achieved your aim. Here you give importance to your own opinion about success.

Second type of success is when you achieve everything

which according to people is success. In this type, you give more importance to people's opinion about success. As per the social dogma, man believes that success means having a big house, plush office, high-flying job or business, luxury cars, and rich or popular friends, without which life is a failure…"

"I too want all of that. That's why I am studying engineering."

"I am not implying that attaining all of that is wrong. Now suppose you score well in exams, you get a fat pay package, and after that you buy all that money can buy. Then? What would you do after that?"

"I guess I'll get married and settle in life, as everyone does."

"Then?"

"I'll have kids. 😊"

"Then?"

"Well, with all this, I'll lead a happy life."

"So, you mean to say all those who have all of this are happy in their lives?"

"Well, maybe all of them are not happy but that's what everyone dreams of."

"That's the irony. Even after achieving all that, one feels a vacuum within. Complete satisfaction and fulfillment is missing. However, people still ignorantly believe those things to be the only measure of success."

"Do you mean to say it's the society that has labeled it as 'success'? But there's something more?"

"Yes. People are so lost in trying to achieve so-called success that they don't even take a pause to rethink about it. They feel that what they see around them is the only way to lead a successful life. For instance, you may feel that being popular in college, having popular friends, maintaining friendship with them, going for parties and picnics, following the latest trends in fashion and having the latest gadgets is success."

"Of course! I don't know any other type of success."

"But have you thought about the fact that the popular friends you're trying to maintain friendship with, most probably won't be with you after college? You may be doing so many things today to please them or to fit in, including some wrong practices like smoking, drinking, partying, lying to your parents, teachers as well as your classmates to maintain your image. Some even bully others, try to pull others down, indulge in shoplifting, etc. All this for people who are going to be with you for only a short time! And the activities you indulge in may have some disastrous or even long-term consequences on your life and career... Have you ever felt deep inside that you don't want to do all of that?"

"Well... yes, I have. Most of the times, I don't feel happy and content trying to follow the 'norm'. But I don't have any other option and I try to cope up with the circumstances around me."

"You don't feel content because somewhere inside, you know there is something more than that kind of success."

"And what's that?"

"Success as per the will of God (or the Universal Self, Allah, Lord, Supreme Consciousness or whatever name you want to give it). This is the third type of success. This kind of success is when you fulfill your purpose of coming to Earth. This is the success you must strive to achieve and the rest will come to you automatically. This is the only success that gives you complete satisfaction and fulfillment."

"Wow! That's deep. I didn't know this. But tell me, what is my purpose of coming to Earth?"

"The purpose of every human being on Earth is to realize

one's true nature, get established in that state, and express the qualities of the true self."

"What's our true nature or true self?"

"Your true self or true nature is formless and limitless. You are divine. The reality is that every one of you is a divine being and hence SUCCESS IS YOUR NATURE. The Universe has programmed each and every individual for success. Everything including love, health, wealth, joy, peace, success, etc. is automatically flowing towards you. You just have to identify and remove what is blocking this natural flow."

"What?! I am a divine being and success is my nature? How's that possible?"

"It's the truth, whether you believe it or not. If you don't believe it and don't remove the blocks, you will continue as you are today. No harm done, right? 😊 However, if you believe it and remove the blocks, then abundance and success shall come flowing to you."

"What blocks?"

"Each one has to identify one's own blocks, which could be negative thinking, fear, worry, insecurity, dullness of intellect, laziness, etc. What do you think is the major block that is preventing you from achieving success?"

"I don't know, let me think. Umm... I don't think I am dull, in fact I feel I'm quite intelligent. I do have some negative thinking, I sometimes feel a bit insecure, and sometimes I don't feel very active..."

"So, what is your major block? Is it... laziness?"

"Listen! I AM NOT LAZY. I sleep late and hence I wake up late at times. That doesn't mean I am lazy! I HATE it when anybody says that."

"I'm sorry... I didn't mean to upset you. And I totally agree that:

You are not lazy."

"You do?"

"Yes. You are not lazy. Laziness or lethargy is not your tendency. It's the tendency of your body-mind. You are much more than your body-mind. As I said, you are an incredibly powerful, divine being. Your true nature is full of zeal, brimming with energy."

"Is it?! That's amazing."

"Yes, it is. Since you are not your body-mind, then any tendency that it has, can be eradicated, so that your divine self can express itself freely. You can then explore the unlimited potential lying hidden within you."

"I would love that!"

"Wonderful. Once you are aware of your major block, you can take steps for eliminating it. Laziness is a self-defeating habit that sets you up for failure. That's the prime reason I haven't shown up in many people's lives."

"Oh, that's bad… but it's not that easy to get rid of laziness."

"I know it's not that easy, but it's not that difficult too. If you really want to and if you decide to get rid of it, nothing can stop you from achieving success. As I told you, success is your true nature. You can't stay away from it for long. Just bringing to light the various forms of lethargy helps you to start getting rid of it. When you consistently practice some powerful techniques that I shall tell you, you will eventually find that the wall of laziness has shattered and the divine qualities hidden behind it (which have always been present) have begun to shine. Then, if you wish, you too can easily have a trophy in your hand… your own trophy. 😊"

"Oh, sorry, I don't know what I was thinking! I'll return it as soon as we are done."

"Good. So let's energize you to get rid of lethargy. To begin with, let's have a glimpse of what lethargy will make you do.

> A middle-aged lady on her way to work would often notice a young man lying under a tree. The young man did not seem to do anything other than lie there and stare at the sky all day long. The lady often wondered how he could afford to do nothing.
>
> One day she couldn't resist and finally approached the young man with her question. "Why do you lie here like a log? Why don't you find some work?"
>
> The young man frowned. "What will I gain by working?"
>
> "If you work, you will start earning money. Then you can buy a house and fill it with comforts and luxuries. You can fulfill all your responsibilities as well."
>
> "Then what happens?"
>
> "You can then lead a life of leisure."
>
> The young man was amused. "I'm already doing that right now. So why do I need to make all that effort?!"

"But, isn't he right?" said Ankit.

"Absolutely not! This story illustrates how laziness dulls an individual's thinking. He thinks, 'Why should I trouble myself if I can get by without putting any effort?' However, success is about the satisfaction you get from achieving what you had decided. But laziness gives him every reason to avoid work. It makes him twist the noble philosophies to suit his lethargic tendency and on top of that he feels that he's great. Since he makes a habit of not completing any work on time, he faces failure and ends up with a life of deprivation and misery..."

"That doesn't sound good."

"It's not. With this tendency, he's going to waste his days until one day he's an old man and then he'll regret thinking, 'What have I done with my life?' At present you're young, you're probably not thinking about that day, but the thing is, laziness actually accelerates time. That's because if you spend most of your time in lazing away, then there's hardly any time left for other activities. One day you're going to wake up and wonder, 'Where did all that time go?!'"

"That would feel terrible!"

"Let's not allow that to happen. I'm here for you right now. If you procrastinate and put me off, I might never come back. You've got the energy and the zest right now! Take life by the wheel and drive it where YOU want to. Don't let indolence become your way of life. It creates habits that you'll wish you never had, like postponing, lying, blaming others, making excuses and many more. Where will these habits lead you? About as far away from me as you can get! The thing is, my friend, you have to own your life. You and only you are the creator of your life."

"You're right."

"And you got to understand the disastrous effects of lethargy. Not only does lethargy come in the way of your material success, it also impedes your spiritual growth. It makes you dense and ignorant. It pulls you away from your innate, radiant nature and consumes you into a senseless existence. There's a difference between existing and living. Which one sounds more interesting and exciting to you? Which one makes you feel alive?"

"Living, of course. I want to live, not just exist."

"Good! Then it's essential to understand that the habit of laziness becomes a tendency that not only impacts your life here on Earth, but also stays with you in your afterlife. With so many aspects I spoke about, I am just trying to show you how it blocks my way from all directions. There is much more to catch on about lethargy. It would be interesting to know in detail how it grips you and makes you do all that which you would never do otherwise. You would learn how easy and fun it is to shed it. I can help you do that. This will open the doors for the most awesome life you can imagine!"

"I would love that!"

"Yes, you would. And you may be surprised to know that lethargy isn't all bad. You don't want to get rid of it completely, but you want to find a balance and use it to recharge your batteries, so that the rest of your time is spent on creating awesomeness."

"Wow! Tell me how to do that."

"Certainly, but don't you think it's enough for today?"

"Enough?! No way. You were going to tell me how I can be successful too!"

"I will, I will, cool down dude. Your family will soon be here. How about we have a little chat every day, say for about 15 days?"

"I'm ready. What time?"

"How about half an hour before you usually wake up?"

"Oh, I know what you're doing… That's clever!"

"And you're smart. So, are you going to be lazy about getting rid of laziness, or do you accept this challenge?"

"Ok…Ok. It's do or die for me; even my exams are approaching. Fine. I accept this challenge. And I SHALL WIN."

"That's exactly what I want! And, one last thing, why don't you google some quotes on laziness and read one or two every day for inspiration?"

"Well, if you insist, I can do that."

"I think it's a good idea. So, let's call it a day. Good night and see you tomorrow morning."

"Yes! Let's begin our chat officially tomorrow morning."

✹ ✹ ✹

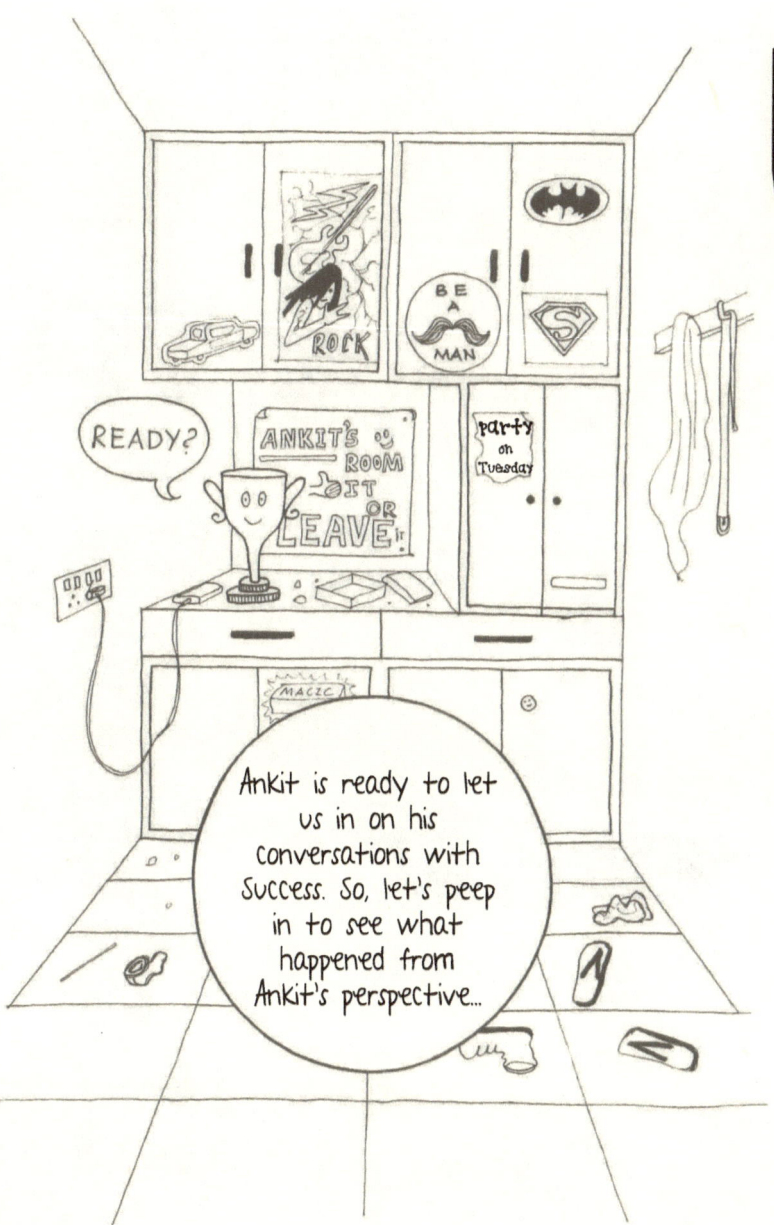

QUOTES

A little knowledge that acts is worth infinitely more than knowledge that is idle.

~ Khalil Gibran

Tomorrow is the only day in the year that appeals to a lazy man.

~ Jimmy Lyons

CONVERSATION 1

Though it was quite difficult, I managed to wake up early the next morning to speak with Success. *Speak with Success?* Have I totally gone nuts? Hope not. But I need to confirm.

Me: Hi, Success! Can you hear me? I hope I wasn't daydreaming yesterday... You spoke to me last night and you're going to speak to me now, right? HELLO!!!

Success: Hello dear and good morning! I'm so happy you have kept your word. And never doubt me; I am here for you—now and always.

Me: Oh, I am so glad to hear your voice again! You are the bestest; no wonder everybody is crazy about you. Also, thank you so much for talking to me yesterday. I wished for you and you heard my call. It kind of blows me away that you listened!

Success: Well, I have always wanted to be with you. In fact, I want to be a part of everybody's life. But some blocks prevent me from appearing. I could now appear in your life because I felt you are ready to get rid of your block.

Me: I guess I am. And I get what you are saying about laziness. When you said that I'm not lazy but basically full of energy and zeal, I felt wonderful. It also piqued my curiosity that if my actual nature is so wonderful and lively, then why don't I experience it all the time? How come it's so hard sometimes to get up the mojo to do anything?

Success: It does feel incredibly great to experience your true Self, which is what I mean about feeling alive and purposeful. But before I jump to the answer of your question, I have some interesting stuff to share with you. It will help you to understand the big picture and set the foundation for your understanding. May I?

Me: Sure, please go ahead.

Success: Great, then let's begin. I told you that your body is lazy, not you, right? Here's how that works: Each body has three basic attributes or *gunas*:

1. Passivity or *tamoguna*, the function of which is rest.
2. Hyperactivity or *rajoguna*, the function of which is action.
3. Equanimity or *sattvaguna*, the function of which is balance between passivity and hyperactivity.

All three attributes are essential in every body. However, usually one of the attributes predominates and makes an individual lethargic, hyperactive or equanimous respectively. The ideal situation is when you have gone beyond all the three attributes to your real self. In that situation all the three attributes are present in the proper proportion and the real you can use each attribute in the right amount at the right time. This would be the attributeless state or *gunateet avastha*.

Me: Whoa! I can see this is going to be an interesting discussion. Am I getting some kind of ancient knowledge or what?

Success: I don't think it really matters whether something is ancient or modern. What matters is how significantly it impacts our life. What do you think?

Me: Hmm... I think you're right. So, how do these attributes impact us?

Success: When the *tamoguna* or passivity predominates in an individual, there is lethargy, heaviness, denseness, darkness, ignorance, delusion, attachment, resistance to change, and inability to meditate because of laziness or getting lost in imagination. Plus everything that we discussed about it yesterday.

Me: Oh, is it the worst of the three?

Success: Unfortunately, it is. Now let's see what happens with the second one. When the *rajoguna* or hyperactivity predominates, there are excessive desires, ambitions, distractions, restlessness, selfishness, aggressiveness, attractions, longing, great expectations of a particular kind of result and reward and power, swinging between extremes of happiness and sadness, and inability to meditate because of restlessness.

Me: It seems better than passivity but still it's not the ideal, is it?

Success: No, it isn't. Hence, let's take a look at the third attribute. When *sattvaguna* or equanimity predominates, there is balance, focus, alertness, knowledge, interest, efficiency, creativity, lightness and joy in everything, and one can easily meditate in depth.

Me: Oh, that means sattvaguna is the best!

Success: It is certainly better and higher than the other two. In fact, it is the launch pad for enlightenment. But there may be internal arrogance or superiority complex about being good and balanced in an equanimous person, because he is not aware of the supreme truth. Hence, one needs to go beyond all the three attributes—to the attributeless state.

Me: Oh, now I understand somewhat.

Success: That's good. Now we will delve further into the three attributes. You know, we can easily identify an individual's predominating attribute based on his or her likes and dislikes. As they have different activity levels, they also have different lifestyles and preferences in food, songs, hobbies, philosophies and even sayings. Inactive people like junk food, stale food, fried food and other heavy foods, which increase inertia. Hyperactive people like hot and spicy food because it gives them extra energy. Equanimous people like pure and wholesome food and prefer vegetarian food. Take a look at your own eating habits and that will give you a clue about your disposition. "You are what you eat" as they say.

Me: I got your point; but everyone likes junk food!

Success: But not everyone goes for it.

Me: Now that you said that, I remember I have seen some people avoiding it as far as possible.

Success: True. So that's the choice they make regarding food. The next point is that their disposition also affects their take on noble philosophies. They put their own twist on the philosophies to suit their tendency.

Me: Oh, really?! How do they twist the philosophies?

Success: Let me give you an example for all three types of people. There is a well-known couplet by the Indian mystic-poet Kabir, that says:

Do tomorrow's work today, and today's work right now. Should the next moment never arrive, then how will your work be completed?

Lazy people twist this and say:

"Do today's work tomorrow, and tomorrow's work the day after. What's the rush when we have so many years to live?!"

Me: 😁 I'm always scheming about how to do today's work tomorrow and get away with it!

Success: Gotcha! 😁

Now let's see what hyperactive people have to say. They say,

"Do day-after-tomorrow's work today, and tomorrow's work right now. Should the next moment never arrive, then how will your work be completed?"

This is what they say because they always need to be busy. They are constantly on their feet. The disadvantage is that because they're always looking ahead, they never enjoy the present moment.

Me: You're right. But let me tell you, it's fun to twist the philosophies.

Success: Yes, it appears interesting and could be fun for a moment. But you should not let it dominate your actions and mislead you from your goal.

Me: Fine. Now tell me about the third category. What's their philosophy?

Success: Equanimous or balanced people who balance perfectly between lethargy and hyperactivity say,

"Do tomorrow's work today and today's work right now. Should the next moment never arrive, then how will your work be completed?"

Me: Hey, it means they don't twist it. That's great!

Success: Yes, but wait. Before you make any judgment, there's more to it. While an equanimous individual has got the saying right, he may be assuming himself to be the doer of the work. This is ego and this tendency of the mind blocks the natural flow from the Self. The Self, the Source or the divinity within us is the actual doer. The body is not the doer! If a person thinks it's the body that does everything, then he is under a great illusion. It's like saying that your car is driving you. No. YOU are driving; the car is just a vehicle, just as the body is the vehicle that the real you—the formless and limitless Self—uses to express yourself here in the physical world.

Me: Whoa!! That's something new! Actually you had mentioned something about this yesterday but I understand this better today.

Success: Good. It's crucial to understand this, as this is the TRUTH. What people have assumed so far is that the body is the doer. This is a false belief and an illusion. To break this illusion, one has to rise from passivity to hyperactivity, from hyperactivity to equanimity, and finally from equanimity to the true Self—which one truly is. One has to transcend all three attributes in order to realize one's original nature.

The equanimous person is heading towards this supreme state, but he still balances hyperactivity and inactivity to serve his ego. The one who transcends all three attributes attains the supreme state which is untouched by these attributes. From this pure attributeless state, one can use the attributes to allow divinity to express itself easily through the body. If you remember, this is the ultimate success or the third type of success that we had discussed yesterday.

Me: Oh, yes! And this is really higher wisdom!!

Success: It is. What you need to understand is that attaining the supreme state is the ultimate aim of every individual who is born on Earth—whether one is aware of it or not.

Me: Mine too?!

Success: Most definitely.

Me: And I can achieve it too?!

Success: Yes, you can.

Me: That's mind-boggling. But that means I should know everything about this subject. So, let's continue. What you were saying is that the equanimous individual's philosophy may appear similar to the one who has achieved the supreme state, but their motivations are different? One is driven by his individual ego, while the other is inspired by the innate divinity?

Success: Exactly. Therefore, to break this illusion, just ask yourself, "The work that I am doing—why am I doing it? And whose expression is this work? Is it the expression of the ego or of divinity?" You have to understand whether the couplet is being used by the ego to achieve its own ends, or it is being used to carry out the work of the higher self.

Me: Okay. I think I understand. So, if I magically ascend and become attributeless, how would I use this saying?

Success: You would say to the unlimited Self, "Whatever

You want me to do today will be done toay, whatever You want me to do tomorrow will be done tomorrow. Thy will is my will." As your thinking would have changed, so would the quote!

Me: So this means that I would be serving the higher self just like the Buddha, Jesus and other messengers of God, right?

Success: Precisely. The one who is established in the Self and experiencing the attributeless state knows very well when the Self has decided to complete a given task. So, being completely surrendered to the Self, he says, "Get the work done today or tomorrow, thy will is my will." By abiding in the Self, he knows what to do and when. He alone can see the entire divine play of the universe and the intricacies involved.

In other words, he knows which key of the piano he should press to produce which note. This is because he can see the entire composition; whereas the lazy, hyperactive and equanimous people can see only a part of it. While playing out the entire composition, one note is played after another. To create the grandest composition, if tomorrow is the perfect time to play a particular note, it should not be played today and vice-versa.

Remember, common sense goes a long way in performing tasks in the right manner and at the right time. When we say, "Do tomorrow's work today," the literal meaning is to finish tomorrow's tasks today. It's a good habit. However, if you don't have adequate information to finish the work today, you will have to put it on hold, until you gather the information. This is common sense. When you are applying common sense, you are essentially letting the Self guide you.

This knowledge helps you understand the attributeless

state and abide in it. Thereby, you keep yourself away from the traps of laziness, hyperactivity and equanimity.

Me: These are pretty subtle differences.

Success: Agreed. Moreover, you cannot distinguish these states externally. Lazy people may appear to be similar to their attributeless counterparts. Both look cool and calm externally. And you might wonder how someone could be so peaceful and stress-free, despite having so much work to do. If the attributeless is sitting in *samadhi* (meditative trance state), it may appear that he is inactive. However, he is not inactive like a lethargic person who is in stupor. He is stabilized in the experience of Self. The difference between the two states is internal—the feeling and understanding with which one functions—rather than external.

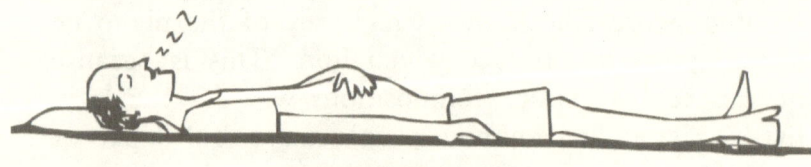

Lethargic State

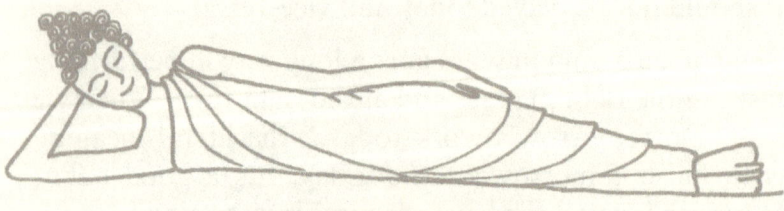

Attributeless State

Me: Looks are definitely deceiving!

Success: They are!

Me: You have been speaking about our true nature, the Self. But, why can't I experience it?

Success: This is because your true nature is masked by these three dispositions. You identify yourself with these dispositions and feel limited. You feel that doing something is too much of a trouble; or, you might feel that you want to do it but have too much on your plate; or, you might want to do it but with the wrong attitude. None of these will allow divine expression to take place. Only the attributeless fully allows divinity to express through his or her body!

Every human being comes to Earth with the aim of attaining this divine state, also known as the *gunateet* state.

Me: I didn't know that I came to Earth with this aim!!

Success: Most people are not aware of this. The reality is that every individual's ultimate aim is to achieve this divine state. In this state, you use each of the three dispositions in the right proportion at the right time. You rest when you need rest—unlike hyperactive people who cannot sit at one place even for a moment. But then you begin working again as soon as you are sufficiently rested—unlike lethargic people who rarely stop resting. And after finishing your work, you easily move on, and are not worried about its result or bothered about getting credit for it—unlike equanimous people whose achievement may be ego-driven. You make use of the available resources, but do not get attached to them. You easily detach yourself from those resources once they are no longer required. Even laziness or passivity is used as a resource in the form of sleep to energize the body; but you cast it aside once it has achieved its purpose of reenergizing the body. So passivity can also be put to use for a higher purpose. It is only the excess passivity which poses a hurdle.

Me: Ah! This makes my job easier. This means I only have to work on eliminating excess passivity and learn to use it like a tool.

Success: True. And when you shed the excess passivity, you automatically experience the zeal and sense of vitality, the feeling of being alive. That's the feeling of the Self, expressing itself through your body! Do you want to experience it?

Me: Yes, I want to.

Success: Splendid. Then here you are. After every conversation, I have some easy steps for you which will bring you closer to me and allow you to experience your true nature. So get ready and dive into the experience of your beingness!

TALK TO YOUR SELF

Dear _____,

(write your name above)

What difference would it make in my life if I attain the attributeless state?

_____
_____
_____
_____
_____
_____
_____

writing is fun

GIVE SELF-SUGGESTIONS

Try talking yourself into action! Here are some suggestions.

Your body listens to whatever you say. It doesn't argue with you. It always acts as you want it to. It won't be an exaggeration if it's said that you can make yourself sick and tired just by saying, "I am sick and tired." But instead, let's focus on the positive side. If you want to free yourself from sluggishness and feel enthusiastic throughout the day, start giving positive suggestions to yourself right from today. Such as:

"I am always active, energetic and enthusiastic."

Self-suggestion is a powerful technique as it programs your subconscious mind. This can help you develop your personality, build a strong character, achieve success, and transform your life.

To get maximum benefit from this technique, you can follow these steps:
- Sit in a comfortable posture. Loosen up your body.
- Tell yourself, "These suggestions will have a positive impact on my mind, body and

environment. All these suggestions are going to manifest into reality very soon." Repeat this before and after the suggestions.

- Give the positive suggestions in a peaceful state with your mind cool and calm, since this is the state in which your receptivity is higher. Have complete faith and understanding about your real nature (unlimited, omnipotent and full of life) while giving these suggestions.

- Give the self-suggestions slowly with feeling and love. For example, if your suggestion is, "I am always active, energetic and enthusiastic," feel the activeness, energy and enthusiasm in your body. Feel the love for your body as it is God's gift to you.

- You get faster results if the suggestions are given in a rhythmic tune. If possible, you can record the self-suggestions in your voice and listen to them as often as possible.

- Initially, practice this every day before going to bed and as soon as you wake up in the morning.

- Be consistent in your practice to gain mastery over this technique. Then you can also practice it while taking a walk or a shower. (You can also talk yourself into some cool dance moves.)

Here are some positive self-talk phrases that will help you to experience and express your true nature.

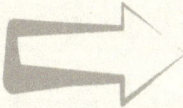

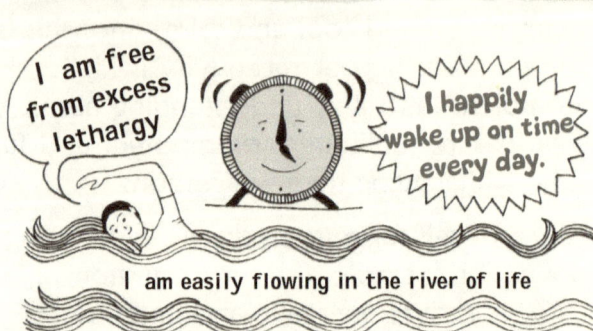

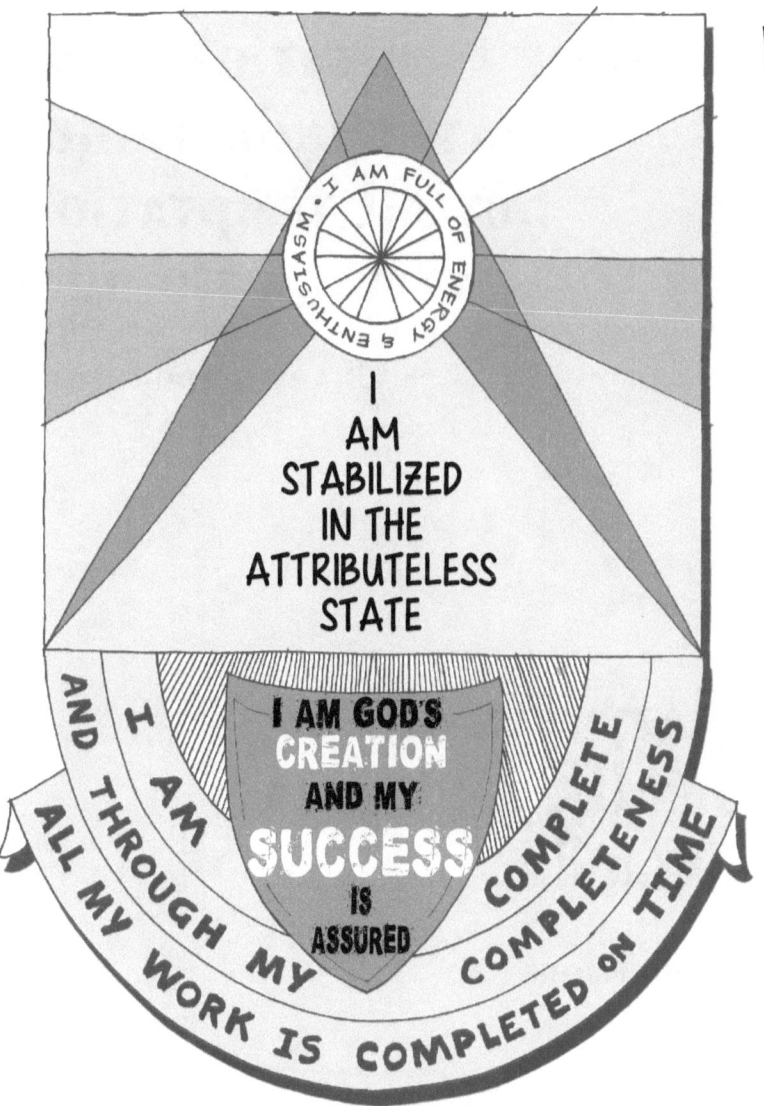

QUOTES

Some temptations come to the industrious, but all temptations attack the idle.

~ Charles Spurgeon ~

A lazy man sleeps soundly, and goes hungry!

~ Anonymous ~

CONVERSATION 2

Me: Good morning, Success!

All that stuff you told me yesterday is awesome. What I understood is that my everyday life serves as a mirror to reflect the governing tendency of my body, right? So if I change my governing tendency, the mirror is going to show me a successful person instead of a lazy bum!

Success: You got it! 😄 And a great morning to you too!

Me: 😄 So, tell me more about a lazy person's lifestyle. It will give me a clue about what I need to abstain from.

Success: Oh, so you want to peep into the life of a lazy person? Then let's visit a lazy person's house in the morning.

The clock shows 8:00 a.m. Typically, a lazybones' brain is not active enough in the morning to think of a good enough reason to get up. He can lie in bed all day if you let him!

But eventually as drowsiness begins to reduce, he somehow

manages to get up and sit on the bed. And what does he see?

Me: Let me guess, he sees nothing because his eyelids are still half closed!

Success: Hahaha. That's what you do, right?! So, with those half-closed eyes, he sees the mess he had left last night.

Me: 😬 That is exactly what happens! I wake up and see all of my unfinished business lying around!

Success: 😬 Then peeping through the blanket, his first thought is: "Ugh! I have to clean up this mess... I have to take a bath... I have to get ready for class..." Then he throws off his blanket and, to feel active, turns on the radio or the TV, or picks up his cell phone. He notices that his cable TV is not working because he hadn't paid the bill. "Oh! I should have done that last week," he thinks. Soon his mind runs over the list of all the other things he's been putting off. He begins to feel guilty. But soon, habit kicks in, and he dives into the pool of excuses for all the tasks he has left incomplete, and thinks, "No harm done. I'll get all this stuff done this weekend."

In this way, he absolves himself of all wrongdoing, and feels relaxed and happy... as if he has finished those tasks! However, this is all in fact a trick of his lethargic mind.

Me: And 'this' weekend never shows up, right?

Success: 😬 No, it never shows up! You've probably experienced this too: Let's say you urgently need to go to the bank for some purpose. But you don't feel like driving to the bank. You start feeling guilty about your laziness, but suddenly you realize: "Oh, today is a bank holiday, so the bank is closed!"

NO LAZY PHILOSOPHY PLEASE!

This thought instantly relaxes you, as if you have already finished your task! However, the task remains unfinished and you'll have to deal with it tomorrow. You know that you have to execute that work to accomplish it, but every time you procrastinate, you give your mind a temporary feeling of accomplishment! But that task hangs over your head until it's actually done.

A lazy individual falls prey to procrastination by using every excuse to take the edge off his guilt and make himself feel good.

This repeats every day and his whole life becomes a cycle of ignoring work, feeling guilty and then making excuses in order to feel better.

Me: I know, it's like when you finally finish something, you can get it out of your head. Otherwise it's always gnawing at you in the background and you are never at peace.

Success: You got that right! Now let's look at a lazy person's eating habits.

Me: I know, he would prefer to have cold, stale food rather than a fresh, hot meal.

Success: Yes. And every time he does this, he increases his inertia. It just gets easier and easier to be lazy. One may wonder, how can people eat stale food? But they like it as it takes them into stupor. Even if they're not hungry, just bored, but to avoid doing anything productive, they eat. Then there are those who live to eat, instead of eating to live. Eating is their preferred pastime!

All this augments the indolence in the body and mind. Indolent people prefer to eat junk food or restaurant food rather than home-cooked meals. Their blood flows more towards the stomach to digest the cold or heavy food they have eaten, rather than the brain, and hence they feel sleepy all the time. It can be said that such people eat partly for themselves and partly for their doctors. This is because they are sure to develop health problems with such eating habits and then they have to visit the doctor.

Then there are some people who unnecessarily trouble their bodies in order to make world records and gain some popularity and praise. They participate in eating contests, where the amount of food they eat is simply ridiculous.

Me: Hehe 😀 It's an easy way to become popular.

Success: Yeah, but to what effect?! Anyway, let's take a look at some of their other *interesting* habits too.

Lethargic people desire comfort and luxury all the time. They always try to avoid any sort of effort. Their great philosophy is:

Why run to do something if you can do it walking? Why walk if you can do it standing? Why stand if you can do it sitting? And why sit if you can do it lying down?

A lazy person constantly craves sleep. Even when he wakes up, he thinks about when he can go to sleep next. His first thought on waking up is: "I wish I don't have to leave my cozy bed!" He also wonders why the sun rises and why morning appears. It's a sort of punishment for him!

Me: Ok, you got me there! I admit there are days when I hate the thought of getting up in the morning! But I am not completely lazy. Sometimes I jump out of bed because I get all excited about what the day holds.

Success: That means you are in the in-between state. You are not entirely lethargic, nor are you hyperactive. You sometimes complete your work and sometimes you don't.

Me: That's right. Ok, what else in a person's behaviour says that he is lazy? I mean, I sure don't want people to think I'm one!

Success: Lazy people are complacent, which makes them careless. With time, it is possible that complacency may turn into total carelessness.

Me: Hmmm, that's true. One of my classmates failed his exams even though he was good in studies. At least he knows he failed because of over-confidence. He got cocky! Before the exam, he thought, "I like this subject. I can easily get good grades in it." And so he did not pay as much attention to that subject as he should have. He did not study enough, thinking he knew it all, and so, of course, his exam did not go well.

Success: Actually, there is no such thing as "over-confidence". But this word has become so popular that everybody uses it. People might say his over-confidence led to his failure. However, "carelessness" is the correct word for "over-confidence". This is because, in reality, confidence cannot be "over" or "in excess", just as love cannot be "over" or "in excess."

Me: Wow, that's a light bulb moment 💡! I never thought of it like that!

Success: Basically, carelessness leads to laziness, and laziness in turn leads to carelessness. Lethargic people know that there is so much to be done. They know it is time to get up and get moving. However, they are so tightly bound by indolence that they cannot get into action even if they want to. Then they feel guilty about not getting anything done, but the funny thing is they still won't work on those tasks. They try to ease their guilt by coming up with various excuses or blaming it on the circumstances or people. As soon as they have found a good excuse, they feel happy and relaxed as if the task is completed—while the task still remains incomplete.

Me: So, the life of a lazy person described in two words can be: **"UNFINISHED BUSINESS"**.

Success: Perfect. Now tell me, how can I enter his life if he is busy sleeping and making excuses? How can I come to him if he's overcome with inertia and remains careless? How can I appear, when everything is incomplete in his life?

Me: That's a no-brainer. You're not coming into his life!

Success: I'm not!

✧ ✧ ✧

TRY SOME **STOP EXPERIMENTS**

There are many people who constantly promise to complete certain tasks, and then fail to do so. This happens almost every day. It is important to break this mental habit. Once you gain control over your mind, you will see yourself completing all your tasks on time. Here are some cool tricks to gain self-control.

COOL TRICKS	TEMPTATIONS
	When you are offered two pieces of your favorite, mouth-watering dessert...
EAT JUST ONE AND LEAVE THE OTHER.	

These small "stop" practices will go a long way in helping you to gain control over your mind. If you can make yourself STOP whenever you want, you can quickly break any unconscious habits that you have.

QUOTES

God gives every bird its food, but He does not throw it into its nest.

~ J.G. Holland ~

Idleness is sweet, and its consequences are cruel.

~ John Quincy Adams ~

Industry adds prosperity. indolence brings but poverty.

~ Thiruvalluvar ~

CONVERSATION 3

Me: Good morning, Success! Today I want to ask in all seriousness, is lethargy that dangerous?

Success: Good morning to you too. And yes, lethargy doesn't look that dangerous, isn't it? Hence, let's take a look at a little story.

> *Once upon a time, there was a little sparrow that lived in a jungle. Each morning, she flew out in search of insects to eat. She would sing and fly about the whole day. Once, a farmer who was passing by the jungle, heard her beautiful song, and praised her lavishly. The sparrow was pleased. She asked the farmer, "Where are you going?"*
>
> *"I am going to the market to sell this box of insects so that I can buy a feather," he replied. The sparrow was excited. "Oh! Why don't you give me that box? I will give you a feather in exchange. I have many feathers. This will save my energy since I wouldn't have to wander in search of food."*

CONVERSATION 3

The farmer happily agreed to the deal, since his energy would be saved as well. The sparrow plucked one feather and gave it to the farmer in return for the box of insects. She was delighted that she could get her food without any effort.

The next day, she was waiting for the farmer. As soon as she saw him, she flew to him and gave him one feather right away. The farmer gave her the box of insects. This continued for many days, until a day came when the sparrow had no feathers left. Hence, the deal could not continue. Also, she was now unable to fly about in search of food. As a result, she died of hunger.

Cute little story, right?

Me: Uh-oh! This means lethargy is very dangerous.

Success: You will realize this only if you think about its consequences. Otherwise, you'll happily give away your hours to lethargy, just like the sparrow gave away its feathers to the farmer. And very soon, you will be left with nothing but regret.

Me: Grave consequences. Not a very comfortable topic.

Success: True, but don't you think it's better to be careful now than to be sorry later?

Me: I agree. So, now what should I do?

Success: Think about all the things you could accomplish in life if you never entertain laziness.

Me: That's a fabulous topic. Let me think... if my body-mind did not make any excuses, I think I could do everything that I want to! I want to excel in studies as well as in sports. I want to be good at dance as well as I would like to be the students leader. I would love to spend quality time with my family as well as have fun with my friends. In the long term, I would have a great career and a fabulous life. Wow!! How awesome my life would be!

PERFORMANCE	GOOD	BETTER	BEST
STUDIES			✓
FRIENDS			✓
SPORTS			✓
DANCE		✓	
FAMILY			✓
EVERYTHING	✓		

WHAT IF
I NEVER ENTERTAIN LAZINESS...

Success: Yes! An awesome life awaits you if you can leave your favorite couch.

Me: I know, and this is not just a pipe dream. I have seen some of my fellow students achieve it all. And I have always envied them.

Success: You too can become the object of envy. Ok, now tell me what opportunities have you missed due to laziness? What great experiences now belong to someone else?

Me: That's a painful topic. I would rather not talk about it, because I think there have been quite a few missed opportunities...

CONVERSATION 3

Success: Even though you wouldn't like to talk or think about it, but still do it, so that you can identify your enemy, which you have taken to be your dearest friend. You have made laziness your constant companion, but you got to see how it robs you of your ability to achieve and prevents you from reaching your highest potential.

Me: That's a huge loss! This BFF is quite treacherous, but its company feels so harmless and soothing and just sooo good!!

Success: Exactly. Let's consider an example. A lady was engrossed in her work. She suddenly turned to her little son and asked, "There was a cake on that table; where is it? Did you eat it?!" The child innocently replied, "I didn't mean to, Mom. I was only trying to smell it. I didn't realize when it stuck to my teeth and then it got finished."

Me: I don't get this one. How is eating the cake equal to being lethargic?

Success: This example illustrates how lethargy sucks you in, even if you are just trying to take a little sniff. For instance, a person says he wants to snooze for just 10 minutes and ends up sleeping for hours, because he does not realize how time flew by. He wakes up early in the morning, but keeps going back to sleep for "five more minutes." Soon, sleep engulfs him, just like the cake tempted the child who just wanted to smell it.

In a nutshell, you remain in danger of being sucked into lethargy until you attain the attributeless state.

Me: I definitely don't want to get sucked into lethargy. It's like a black hole that would never let me out!

Success: That's right. Every creature on this planet has been given a body in order to work. One should rest only when tired. Those who shirk and look for shortcuts will eventually realize that the supposed shortcut wasn't a shortcut at all, but a path that invites bigger problems.

It is due to lethargy that a person postpones today's work to tomorrow. It is due to lethargy that he avoids effort. It is due to lethargy that he does not want to exercise his body. As a result, his body becomes weak, obese and susceptible to diseases.

All in all, man has to liberate himself from laziness since it is a major mental ailment in itself. Everyone needs to contemplate on this topic. The example of the sparrow would have helped you to realize the present and future consequences of laziness in your life.

Me: In a big way!

Success: Contemplation on consequences indeed takes you a long way. You may be able to save yourself from laziness while there's still time. Otherwise, the human mind is wired in such a way that you feel like doing only those things that you like. Repetition of this practice programs your subconscious mind in such a way that it becomes your habit. And your habits are either going to push you in the right direction or wrong direction, or keep you stuck at the same place—making you stagnant.

Me: That's bad... but I don't always look at the big picture of consequences. I tend to go for instant gratification!

Success: Suppose I ask you to imagine how your life would be 12 years from now. In all likelihood, if you continue with your present behavioral patterns, it will be much the same as it is today, or even worse. Think about it: "How would my life be, if everything continues in the same way and at the same speed?" This will get you thinking about the ramifications and how you can change those right now.

You should be clearly able to see what would be the repercussions if you constantly duck out of work. The more clearly you can see and understand that, the better you will perform your job. And the easier it will be to free yourself from this debilitating habit.

To work on this in depth, contemplate on what losses the world has suffered till date due to laziness and what this habit will bring in the future.

Me: That's a huge task! But I shall give it a try.

✹ ✹ ✹

CONVERSATION 3

ASK YOURSELF THESE QUESTIONS

What would I gain by getting rid of laziness? How would my life be without laziness?

- PHYSICAL — E.g.: I would be fit and fine to do all the activities that I want to.
- MENTAL
- SOCIAL
- FINANCIAL
- SPIRITUAL

In which situations do I fall prey to laziness?

- E.g.: I overeat when it's my favorite sweet dish.

WANNA KNOW ABOUT YOURSELF?

WANNA KNOW ABOUT YOURSELF?

ASK YOURSELF THESE QUESTIONS

What are the opportunities I have lost due to laziness?

E.g: I lost the opportunity to be in the cricket team, because I felt lazy to go for practice every day.

- PHYSICAL
- MENTAL
- SOCIAL
- FINANCIAL
- SPIRITUAL

How do I create double trouble due to laziness?

E.g: Overeating increases inertia. Also, it leads to obesity which invites ridicule as well as diseases.

QUOTES

Idleness is the dead sea, which swallows all virtues.

~ Benjamin Franklin

If you are
wasting your
time today by
wandering about,
lying around or
indulging in wrong habits,
you are not only losing
a precious opportunity, you are ruining
your life; because you will do the
same thing tomorrow.

~ Sirshree

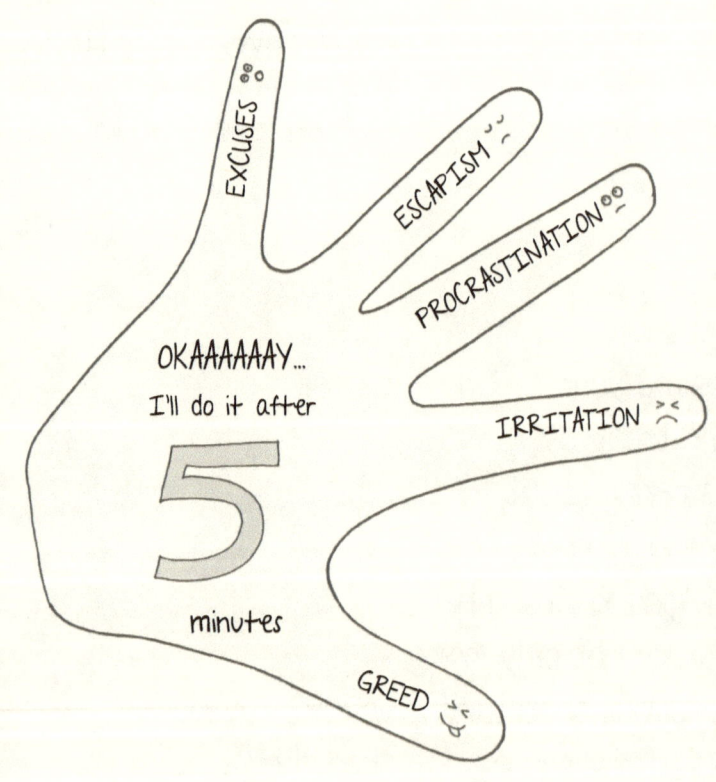

CONVERSATION 4

Me: Good morning, Success!

Success: Very good morning to you too. So how are you today?

Me: I'm fine, thank you. Yesterday I was thinking that lethargy is really sneaky, right? It grips us so silently that we don't realize it until things have already started going wrong for us. So, what are those habits I need to be on the lookout for? I'm going to need a clone of myself to keep up with all of this!

Success: Now, that's dramatic! It's not as hard as you might think. Talking about habits, lethargy paves the way for many wrong habits but with awareness you can catch them.

Me: So, awareness is the mantra?

Success: Yes, it is. Now let's begin our discussion about habits. The first habit of a lazy person is that he avoids responsibility and consequently avoids success. He starts wriggling out of work right from his childhood. As he grows up, this behavior continues. He looks for every reason to shirk his responsibility and is very pleased when he finds one. That's the most harmful habit he adopts, knowingly or unknowingly.

Secondly, he is always eager for relief. He thinks, "I need relief for the time being. I'll see what to do later on." He seeks relief from guilt and unhappiness due to unfinished work—anything to take the edge off, even if temporarily. For example, he calls his family or friends and narrates them his version of events. Typically, they listen and offer him words of solace. This makes him feel better.

Me: Yup, escapism is how I sometimes get out of the bad feeling associated with leaving things undone. But it's easier to say "it wasn't my fault" than to take responsibility.

Success: Yes, it seems easier, but it's also lazier. Thirdly, when a task is to be done, you will often hear him saying, "What's the rush?!"

Me: "Come on, why do I have to do it now? I can do it later." That sounds like me when my mom asks me to do anything!

Success: If this kind of thinking becomes a habit, it will create a deep-rooted tendency of procrastination, and then it will be very difficult to get into action. A lazy person keeps postponing everything: decision-making, planning and action... Basically, he avoids taking any steps that can help him achieve success.

Me: Hmm... That means it's he himself who keeps success away and then blames his fate for his failure.

Success: Precisely. And the fourth point is that if he has become habituated to laziness, he is very likely to indulge in greed as well. He will always want anything and everything that safeguards his lethargy. For instance, he will crave for more sleep and more food; he will make more and more excuses. Then, there is another bad habit you may come across during your interactions with a lethargic person.

Me: What's that?

Success: A lethargic person gets very irritated when disturbed during his rest—which of course is something that he prefers to do most of the time. This is because he does not want any interruptions in his lazy lifestyle. Here is a joke that explains it better.

> *Once a man went and sat on a grave. Soon, he was bored and wanted to smoke a cigarette. He took one out and lit it up. The corpse from the grave shouted, "You, there... Get out of here!" The man took offence. "How conceited of you to not even let me sit here and relax!" The corpse retorted, "Why shouldn't I be conceited? I had to die to earn this spot!"*

It's the same with a lazy person. He always wants to lie around without being disturbed, even

in his afterlife! His favorite inner dialogue is: "I hate being interrupted when I am resting." Given a chance, he won't mind saying this to others.

Me: Ha-ha! I get it. But I don't understand, why has God installed laziness in the human body in the first place? That sounds like a programming error!

Success: Good question. Every car has brakes, but no one uses them all the time. They are used only when needed. Yet you will agree that it is important to have brakes, whether or not you need them at a given time. Just because something is not being used at the present moment, it doesn't mean that you'll never need it in the future. Therefore, you should not discard it from the car's system. A car should possess brakes, not to be applied continually, but to use whenever required. That's the rule.

Likewise, lethargy has a God-given function. It's meant to restore your energy, but you must discard it the moment you're done with it.

Me: You mean to say that, just like I've to learn to use the brakes at the right time in the right way, similarly I have to learn to use passivity in the right manner at the right time. Animals do that naturally, don't they? I can't get over how cats can fall asleep and then pounce on a mouse practically from a deep sleep!

Success: Actually, just like animals, you too should rest when your body gets tired and then simply get up and push aside the indolence when it's time to get into action.

Me: Well, cats do sleep all day 😜! Just kidding, I get what you're saying.

Success: A lazy person would surely envy their lifestyle! Anyway, coming back to the topic, the one who is stabilized in the attributeless state uses this God-given function of lethargy very effectively. He uses resources, but does not get attached to them. When the need is fulfilled, detachment occurs smoothly and easily. This saves him from all kinds of miseries and sorrows.

Me: How do I implement this in practical life?

Success: Be aware in every situation of your life, and when it comes to action, ask yourself, "Am I using passivity effectively or am I letting it control me?" If you are preparing yourself for the highest aim of achieving the attributeless state, you would practice a little in every situation so as to not fall prey to lethargy.

Me: Hmm. That makes sense. So, I need to be aware of five things: 1. Am I making any excuses in order to avoid responsibilities? 2. Am I trying to find some relief? 3. Am I protecting my habit of procrastination? 4. Am I falling prey to greed? 5. Am I developing the habit of irritation due to interruption in my rest?

Ooh! A big list!

Success: That's a good summary. And no, it's not a big list. All you need is a new habit of using indolence effectively. And habits aren't that difficult to create. It's no more difficult to create a positive habit of balancing passivity and activity than it is to create a self-sabotaging habit of laziness. It just takes practice. When you develop this good habit, lethargy and all other negative tendencies will begin to leave your body. You'll then begin to LIVE in the true sense.

Me: So the formula is: Practice, practice, practice.

Success: Yes. Practice of developing good habits.

✼ ✼ ✼

If you are feeling tired after working or studying for some time and feel that you cannot do anymore, ask yourself, "Can I do this for another five minutes?" The answer will be 'yes', always. This is because you clearly know that continuing the work for the next five minutes is not a big deal. These five minutes will help immensely, even though you may not find this technique important or special initially. However, it's a real attitude-changer.

QUOTES

SUCCESS IS RESERVED FOR YOU IF YOU PERSEVERE, DESERVED BY YOU YOU ARE INDOLENT.

— ISRAELMORE AYIVOR

WHO KNEW YOU COULD EVEN BE

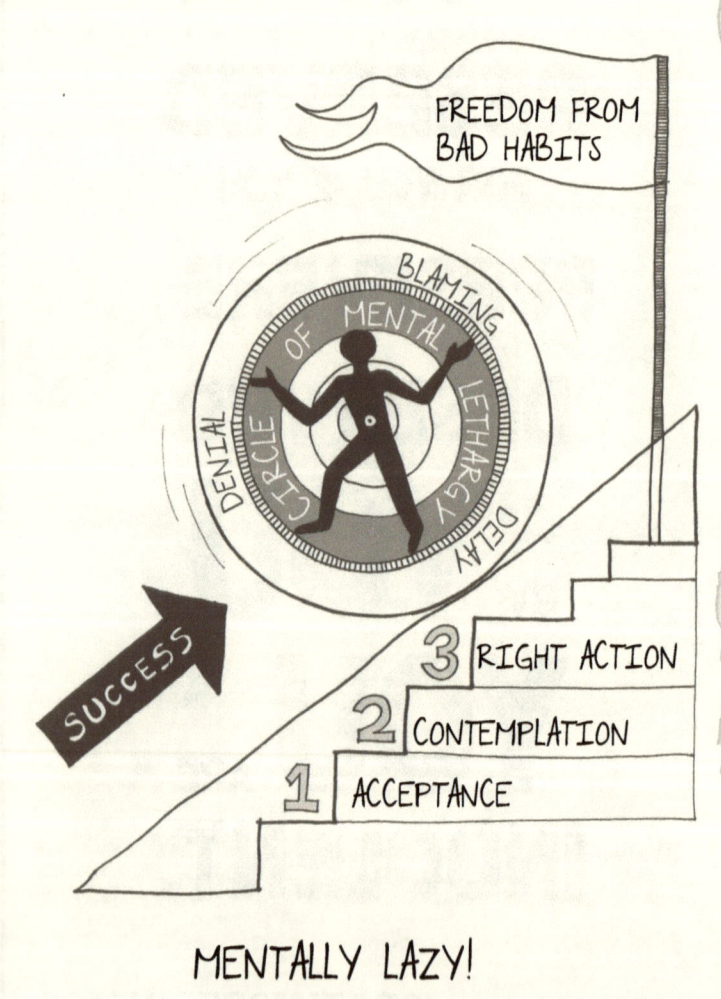

MENTALLY LAZY!

CONVERSATION 5

Me: Good morning, Success! I'm all set to work on eliminating the habits you told me yesterday. I guess we are done with bad habits.

Success: Not really.

Me: What?! Are there any other habits I should be aware of?

Success: There are. So, without wasting any time, let's nip them in the bud right now! People think that sleeping excessively or lying on a couch all day are the only signs of lethargy. However, they fail to recognize lethargy at the mental level.

Me: Mental lethargy? I thought lethargy was a tendency only of the body.

Success: No. Lethargy can exist in every aspect of one's life. Mental lethargy does not allow an individual to think. If given a number of options regarding a particular project, he will pick anything that comes to his mind and say, "Yes, this is fine. Let's do this." He does not feel like thinking about anything and it's almost impossible for him to reflect in depth upon any given subject. When told to contemplate on a certain topic, he would reply, "I know everything.

I don't need to think on anything." He simply refuses to contemplate. Plus, given an option between doing something old and something new, he would always choose the old.

Me: Because doing anything new requires more effort, mentally as well as physically 😕.

Success: Yes. Now consider this: what if you tell a friend of yours that he tends to avoid work? What would most probably be his immediate response? Unless he is honest, he will refuse to accept the criticism or he will ignore it, although he knows perfectly well that whenever he can, he always wriggles out of work. This kind of mental attitude of ignorance or denial is also induced by mental lethargy. It keeps a person from doing the minimal effort of thinking about what's being said to him. He refuses to hear the truth about himself and that keeps him from growing and succeeding.

Me: Nobody likes criticism!

Success: True. But if you are wise, you will listen to constructive criticism. Otherwise, you could end up creating a habit of blaming others and refusing to take personal responsibility. Remember, the universe guides you in your growth by all possible means. It has a way of helping you by giving you certain indications and feedback through people or situations. Hence, take 100% advantage of that feedback without going into the details such as who is the person giving the feedback, what words he/she used or how that person is wrong in his/her own life. Your job is to receive the feedback sportingly and improve yourself. Nature will take care of improvements in that person; you need not worry about that.

Me: So, I shouldn't reject any criticism immediately.

Success: That's right. Also remember that any task that comes to you is sent by the universe as a form of training to prepare you for a higher purpose. For instance, the homework or projects you get in school, college or office is an exercise to sharpen your brain, which will help you excel in the future. Think about how the indications or the tasks sent by the universe today will help you tomorrow.

Me: Oh! What I understood is that any task that comes to me is a help from the universe, with which I can break my comfort zone and stretch my abilities. Right?

Success: Right.

Me: Okay. Now I want to know more about how one gets into the habit of blaming.

Success: Fine. Let's discuss that when a job remains unfinished, a sluggish person denies the criticism, and in order to save himself, puts the blame on someone else. "It's not my fault. It's their fault." Then this blame game leads to delay in the work, encouraging the habit of procrastination.

Me: So, it's denying, then blaming, and then delaying.

Success: That's the chain. These people get very good at convincing themselves and others that they're waiting for some necessary detail to fall into place before they can finish the work. Some even take it so far as to think that if they procrastinate enough, someone will get frustrated enough to get the task done from someone else. This can become a formula for a shirker. Especially in time-bound tasks, other people pitch in, preferring to help, rather than leaving the job incomplete.

Imagine a person who puts off a particular job every day.

One day, he finds someone else has finished it. He thinks, "Wow! It's done, and I didn't have to do anything!" As a result, he repeats this behavior every time he is faced with a task he dislikes.

He starts coming up with more elaborate excuses for not finishing the work, thinking, "If I put it off long enough, someone else will come along and do it."

If you spill water, it will eventually dry.

NO LAZY PHILOSOPHY PLEASE!

He thinks he's being very clever, without realizing that he is, in fact, undermining his aim of achieving his ultimate purpose on Earth—to abide in the true Self and to express its qualities. To achieve this purpose, the body-mind needs to be disciplined to accomplish every kind of work.

Me: You're right. But hey, I don't want to hear anything about discipline! I have enough of that from my parents and professors. It's difficult for many of us, and discipline is boring!

Success: It's not like you think about discipline. Let me tell you something that every student experiences at some point. A student studies extra hard and completes his syllabus in the last few days before his exams. He then thinks, "If I can study so much in the last few days, how much more I could do if I studied all year! Next year,

I will study right from the beginning." Then comes the summer vacation and all these noble thoughts disappear into thin air. Old habits kick in and he thinks, "Why study all year when I can get such good grades after a few days of cramming just before the exams?!"

Me: 😬 Busted! You seem to know all the tricks the lazy mind plays with us. I can't get anything past you, can I?

Success: I've watched this very closely everywhere. Students who think this way do not realize that they are forming a habit of starting work at the eleventh hour. They may finish their tasks, but will probably never discover the joy and satisfaction of completing a well-planned job.

They won't be able to witness the beautiful and better results that careful work can produce. They won't realize that the habit of carrying out jobs in a systematic manner can get them successful results all their life. No one who delays work—be it an actor, scientist or engineer—can ever grasp the full depth of one's field, nor attain the ultimate purpose of life.

Once you taste a planned success, you will never find it boring. Rather it's a wonderful feeling of true achievement.

Me: Well-planned success does sound better, now that you have explained it in that manner. As you had mentioned earlier that success is doing what I have decided to do, then this habit of well-planned success will automatically make me more disciplined.

Success: Right. You should also know that it's okay if you're unable to complete a job once in a while. However, make sure you are not making a habit of avoiding work by delaying it. If you have this tendency, and if you accept that you have it, only then will you work on overcoming it. If you can make yourself complete a task just once, you'll feel great. That task will be out of your hair and you will realize, "This can be done every time. I can feel good about getting things done!"

Me: Is it really that easy to get rid of mental lethargy?

Success: Yes, if you approach it with the right attitude.

The first step is, do not deny it. If someone tells you something about you that you don't like, don't say, "You're wrong, that's not how I operate!" Instead accept it. Others tend to see things about us that we are blind to. Consider that a blessing. It's a gift to be shown a way to improve. Then think about how you can overcome the habit, and when you do overcome it, you can take the next step easily. Nothing can stop you then.

Consider the saying, "A stitch in time saves nine." It means that stitching up a small tear immediately will save you from having to patch up a much larger hole later. Likewise, starting to take small steps against a habit the minute you notice it forming within you will make it easier to uproot it.

Me: You're right. Stronger habits are harder to break.

Success: That's the reason some people struggle all their lives to get rid of bad habits. Don't let that happen to you. Beware!

Me: I will be. So, I shouldn't be so thick-skinned when people clue me into what I'm like. And then, what next?

Success: Next, you have to use the power of contemplation. Contemplate on the feedback you have received and think about how you'll work on it to improve yourself. When you first face a critical situation, contemplate on it to such an extent that when you face a similar problem in the future, you find it easy to make decisions and speedily work on the solution. Only when your contemplation takes place at such a profound level, will it cover even the subtler aspects of the problem. This power of contemplation will help you find a solution to every problem, and make you stronger. Although many people learn from their own bittersweet experiences, but one can also learn without undergoing the negative experience, by using the power of contemplation.

Me: That's right! Contemplation is something that was missing in my life.

Success: Use the power of contemplation to understand the governing tendency of your body. When you contemplate on its consequences, you automatically tend to make the highest choices in life. You choose discipline to complete tasks on time over procrastination. You take necessary actions. This possibility will open up when you take steps to completely liberate yourself from lethargy.

Me: All I need is the right approach. How do I put everything together?

Success: Break this vicious cycle of denial, blame and delay. Then take a new turn in your life with the help of acceptance, contemplation and the right action at the right time.

Me: Great! Then it's freedom from all bad habits!!

✺ ✺ ✺

To break the pattern of denial-blame-delay, you must develop an opposing pattern: the "do-it-now" pattern. If you want to organize your table, don't wait till the weekend—do it now! Just think about how great you'd feel to get things done and have NO unfinished business hanging over your head!

To begin a task is important and to complete it brings satisfaction. Those who complete their work successfully always receive the fruit of satisfaction. You must involve your mind, body and intellect to complete the work that you have undertaken. If you are still unable to accomplish your goal, remember the importance of trying until you succeed. Edison kept on trying until he invented the light bulb. He has been quoted as saying that 10,000 failed experiments served to teach him those many ways in which a light bulb cannot be created. Note that he wasn't discouraged by failure, nor did he give up. Likewise, you too have to strive to give the last punch in order to assure your success.

QUOTES

Goddess Lakshmi favors the hardworking and despises the lethargic who rely on their fate alone.

~ **Panchatantra** ~

Relax a little before you get tired. Start working before you become lazy.

~ **Sirshree** ~

REST IS IMPORTANT... BUT

THERE'S A RIGHT WAY TO REST

AND A WRONG WAY TOO!

CONVERSATION 6

Me: Good morning, Success! I liked the idea of contemplation. And who doesn't love the thought of taking action right away and getting stuff done and out of one's hair. But what about rest? I absolutely need it! Everybody needs a break, even after enjoying the satisfaction of accomplishing their tasks on time! I can't be "go-go-go" all the time.

Success: Of course, rest is important. A couch potato would be so pleased to hear this. He would think, "Aha! That's what I say and that's exactly what I do all day."

However, I need to point out that the rest or repose I am talking about does not mean reclining on a

couch all day. Resting your body means re-energizing it before it gets exhausted. It refers to the tranquility or peace that you feel after killing the demons of the mind like anger, envy, hatred, greed, sloth, lust, and so on. It is the state that is experienced during *samadhi*—the purest form of rest. This is a state of complete awareness of the real Self with pure experience of freedom from all the boundaries made by the human mind for itself.

Remember you are limitless and free from those boundaries. That's your true nature and that's what you experience during deep meditation.

Me: Amazing. I've never heard about anything like this before. Just listening about this kind of rest makes me want to experience that state.

Success: You feel this way because of its glorious nature.

However, lethargic people do the exact opposite. They live in a state of drowsiness, unconsciousness and inactivity, which pulls them away from the purest rest—*samadhi*. Their rest is like that of Kumbhakarna— the mythological demon from the epic *Ramayana*, who used to sleep for six months at a stretch in a year. That's not true rest.

Then there are hyperactive people who have many ambitions and aspirations and hence are always restless and running about. Their rest is like that of Ravana—the demon king from the *Ramayana*, who was always on the move and could not sit peacefully at one place. He always wanted to achieve more and more.

Me: So, one is apathetic and inert, while the other is restless and extremely ambitious. Neither one of them gets proper rest, do they?

Success: No, they don't. What your body needs is balanced rest—like that of an equanimous person who rests before getting tired and gets back to work before feeling lazy.

Me: That's perfect. So, you have to identify that point just before you're drained and take a rest, and then get out of that comfy bed before you get sucked into it for the rest of the day.

Success: :) Excellent! Maintaining this balance gives you a healthy body and a healthy mind. People assume that sleeping more will refresh them more. On the contrary, more sleep causes more laziness.

Me: I always experience this. Whenever I take a long nap in the afternoon, I don't feel energized. Instead, I feel sluggish during the evening and all of my tasks scheduled for the evening are left hanging. It's better if I take a very short nap or no nap at all. But it's hard to resist sleeping in the afternoons on some days!

Success: That's why it is important to get back to work at the right time. When you can identify that "point" as you call it, then you can master the art of using your body optimally.

CONVERSATION 6

Think about this: an average human heart beats 70 times a minute and continues to beat for an average of 70 years. The stomach goes in and out with every breath you take. Do these organs get tired? No. But your hands get tired and your back gets tired.

Me: Wow, you're right! I never thought about that.

Success: Why doesn't the heart get tired? Why do you never hear anyone saying their stomach is tired? This is because the heart and stomach rest even as they work. They expand and contract alternately. Thus, they rest before they get tired.

You need to learn this technique. In everything you do, rest before getting exhausted and then get going again before you get lazy.

And with the help of meditation, give rest to your mind as well.

Me: So, I have to give rest to my body and my mind too.

Success: Yes. Meditation helps you to relax the mind. Perfect relaxation can be attained only if your mind turns inward and comes in contact with the experience of Self within. If your mind falls in love with that experience and gets immersed in its devotion, that is when it attains true peace and calm. Such a mind, freed from demons, will have the most favorable effect on the body. That is true rest.

Me: So, the mind impacts the body in a big way.

Success: Absolutely.

Moving further, when you lean against a wall, you never worry that it may fall down. When you plop down into a rocking chair, you don't worry that it may break.

Me: I don't think anyone thinks that way. When they've to sit, they just sit.

Success: Right. This is because you have complete confidence in the wall or the rocking chair.

Me: Umm... maybe yes. I mean I don't have any doubts on those things.

Success: Right. Likewise, for the mind, there is no greater rocking chair (support and comfort) than the experience of being one with the infinite Self. (This is because the nature of the Self is love, joy and peace.) When you develop this conviction, you can easily hand over all your burdens to Self, God, Consciousness, or whatever name you have faith in. When you develop complete faith in the Self or God, your journey of life will no longer be led by the demons of the mind but, blissfully, by the experience of oneness with God. When that happens, you receive guidance directly from God.

When you have faith, your mind surrenders to the Self or God within you. And when the mind surrenders, it experiences true rest and peace. In this state, even the physical body gets rest.

People tend to think that in today's busy world, it is impossible to find time for rest, and true rest is possible only in the grave.

"Here lies Mr _____. May he rest in peace" is a common epitaph on tombstones. Most epitaphs also have the person's birth and death dates, with a small line in between the two dates. The line could be curvy ~ or it could be a broken line – – – as if the individual had intermittently separated from God. ☺

Me: That's funny! But seriously, what you said about oneness with the Self is so profound. It seems like a person without this sacred knowledge rarely experiences true rest.

Success: You can say that. Even if he experiences it, he won't be able to comprehend it.

Me: Oh. Moving on, how is the rest of a hyperactive person?

Success: Well, a hyperactive person rests so that he can work more later. He can't get his mind off work. He goes to bed at night just so that he can catch some sleep and get back to work in the morning with renewed energy. His only aim is to work and to be on the move. Rest and relaxation are unnatural to him. And that is how he's away from his true self.

Me: He doesn't like to rest and sees it as a waste of time? Incredible!

Success: On the other hand, a lethargic person is constantly looking for excuses to avoid work. And when he forces himself to do any work, it is usually so that people will let him get back to his rest. He engages in tasks only because if he doesn't complete those, people would be hounding him. Sleep is his only aim.

When I was in high school I had two favorite subjects: lunch and recess.

NO LAZY PHILOSOPHY PLEASE!

Me: Hahaha... you always make me laugh when you talk about lethargic people!

Success: It's they who make me laugh!

So, in a nutshell, both lazy and hyperactive people are not in contact with the Self. Their rest is not rest in the real sense.

Me: Actually, I'm a bit confused. How can a body attain rest without becoming lethargic?

Success: We need to ask ourselves whether all our body parts are working like our stomach or heart. No, they are not. In everyday life, we bend only forward and not backward. We also tend to favor one side over the other. Thus, some parts of the body experience too much movement and some parts do not experience any movement at all. This is what leads to aches and pains in the body. If we pay close attention to every part of our body, if we exercise by bending forwards and backwards, and by stretching the sides as well, we can move and relax all parts of the body. This is the basic premise of yoga. *Asanas*, or yoga postures, were specially formulated to bend our bodies in various ways. Most *asanas* force the body to bend in directions in which they usually wouldn't. This relaxes as well as rejuvenates the body. Even deep-rooted inertia can be eradicated by practicing various *asanas*.

In ignorance, people are not able to relax in the true sense. Their bodies do not get rest and their minds do not attain serenity because that is possible only when the mind connects with the infinite Self within. Since that is not happening, there is no question of experiencing well-being, which comes from the Self.

You will be able to give rest to your body only when you please the Goddess of Relaxation.

Me: Goddess of Relaxation?! Did you just make that up? Is there such a goddess? You gotta be kidding me!

Success: 😁 Just listen to this story.

Once a man went to a sage and asked, "What should I do to

attain success?" The sage replied, *"You have to please the Goddess of Relaxation."* The man was astonished by this answer. He had always thought he would need to appease the Goddess of Wealth to achieve sucess, and here was this sage talking about the Goddess of Relaxation! He was puzzled.

So, the sage explained, *"The Goddess of Relaxation is the same as the Goddess of Wisdom (Saraswati). When you acquire wisdom (Saraswati), your intellect opens up, you get the best ideas and do your best work. As a result, wealth automatically comes to you."*

In other words, the sage told the man that when you please the Goddess of Wisdom, then the Goddess of Wealth gets envious and follows you. However, the Goddess of Wisdom is not envious, and so if you please the Goddess of Wealth first, the Goddess of Wisdom will not follow. To be successful, you need to have both in your life. Hence, the smart way to get them both is to please the Goddess of Relaxation first."

Me: I'm guessing that we can't do that by sitting around doing nothing. What's the trick?

Success: You're right! It's about being committed and working sincerely, but in a relaxed state—unhurried intuitive and egoless. That's when the Self within you starts to shine and blossom. The Self remains constricted within you if you harbor negative thoughts like that of greed, sloth, envy, suspicion, anxiety, fear, etc.

People who are balanced have the right understanding about the body. Remember, the body is supposed to be a medium for the Self to experience and express itself. Thus, the body should help in connecting with the Self, rather than separating from it. Only then can the real work of the body begin and then alone can you train your body to relax.

Me: That's huge! I guess I need to relax now… of course in the right way—being one with my true self.

✺ ✺ ✺

ENJOY RELAXATION

Close your eyes and place the palms of your hands on them with love. Then say to them, "Release this stress. Let it go. Relax... relax... relax..." You will be surprised to find the stress in and around the eyes slowly fading away. This is because our body parts listen to us.

You can also use this technique to talk to each and every part of your body into relaxing itself. Some parts of the body take a while to respond. When that happens, just continue repeating the suggestions, "Let this fatigue go. You can relax now. Relax... relax... relax..." They will eventually release all the accumulated fatigue. If you do this, you will relax your body in the actual sense.

RELAXATION MEDITATION

Sit in an appropriate posture for meditation. Adopt a suitable *mudra* of your fingers, for example, the wisdom mudra (*gyan mudra*). In this mudra, you join the tips of your thumb and index finger, while keeping the other three fingers straight.

- Close your eyes. Relax yourself by taking one or two deep breaths and then releasing them slowly.

- Subsequently let your breathing continue normally as it is at present—shallow or deep, comfortable, natural... however it may be, let it continue the same. Don't try to control it. If you control your breathing, then it is not meditation, it is *pranayam* (breath regulation).
- Be aware whether the breath is coming in or going out... now it came in... now it went out... from the right nostril... from the left nostril... or from both nostrils. Be aware of every direction and every state (cold or warm) of the breath.
- Focus your mind on the breath that is coming in and going out. Perceive the breath that is coming in and identify the breath that is going out... it came in... it went out... came in... went out. Just remain aware of your breathing as it is— natural breathing, comfortable and easy breathing.
- Sometimes your breathing will be deep and sometimes shallow. Keeping the body steady, remain aware of the coming and going of every breath. With this you will start feeling calm and composed amidst the constant chattering of your mind.
- Now, in order to relax your mind, you can visualize a natural scene, with your eyes still closed. It may be the one which has been dearest to you.
- Let your eyes wander around in that scene. Pay attention to all the important details in that scene.
- When your mind has seen and experienced the complete scene, then check your body. If there is still some tension in some part of the body, contract it and then let it loose. In this way, release the tension from the arms, legs, shoulders, waist, knees, and eyes.
- You can enjoy this relaxation meditation for 15-30 minutes as per your convenience.

QUOTES

People
do not lack
strength
they lack will

~ Victor Hugo ~

CONVERSATION 7

Success: Good morning, Ankit!

Me: Oh... is it time to wake up already? I don't feel like... but hey, don't call me lazy. I've been waking up early the last few day, isn't it? I hate it when people call me lazy, especially my family members. Ok, so I get up late in the morning sometimes. It's that I cannot get up on time. I try but I fail most of the times. But I'm not lazy. Don't you think it's okay to sleep a little longer in the morning when you're active the rest of the day?

Success: Appropriate amount of sleep is always required, but you should not encourage inertia. I think we shouldn't overlook the harmful effects of oversleeping. If you oversleep for just 30 minutes a day, you're wasting more than 180 hours each year. And sleeping one extra hour each day will cost you 365 hours, or nine 40-hour weeks, each year. So, in a lifetime of about 80 years, you'd be wasting 9 x 80 = 72 weeks of work. That's a lot of time. As it is, we normally sleep away one-third of our lives. Given the amount of creation we could do, do we really need to lie in bed longer than that?

Me: Gosh! I've never done the math on that!

Success: Never underestimate how precious time is. Instead of thinking about the comfort of sleeping an extra hour, think about the satisfaction of achievement if you were to use that hour wisely. Take a pause. Really think about it.

You can use this extra time to do things that you previously did not have the time or energy for. You'll feel wonderful. And when you have time for everything you wish to do, it makes you balanced, relaxed and effective.

Me: But it's really difficult to leave a warm and cozy bed in the morning!

Success: Everyone wants to get out of bed on waking up. But a lazy person cannot get out of bed because he cannot think of a reason to leave his warm, soft bed. His first thought is, "I don't feel fresh yet. Let me sleep for five more minutes. And, anyway, what's the rush? It will take just half an hour to get ready. Then why get up early if I don't need to?" So he tosses around and every day hits the snooze button on his alarm.

I could be a morning person, if morning happened to be around noon.

NO LAZY PHILOSOPHY PLEASE!

Me: Then suddenly it hits him—he's going to be late! He springs into action, freaked out by all he has to do, and ends up running around like a monkey!

Success: You know it well ☺, he shoots up in a panic. "Oh no, it's sooo late!" Having wasted time in that extraa sleep, he now has to race to get ready for his classes or for work. Irritation, clutter, and yelling accompany this hurry.

This has a ripple effect. He is late for everything and has to rush to complete each of his activity on time. This creates stress and tension. All of this could have been avoided had he got up on time!

I know this happens even if one doesn't want it to happen, but ends up doing the same, every time. So, what should be done? Try this simple trick. Before you go to bed, give yourself a rock-solid reason to wake up in the morning with enthusiasm and energy. You'll then find it easier to rise and shine every day. The reason could be anything from attending your favorite class to doing something fun with friends, playing your favorite sport to contributing to a social cause. For spiritual people, attending discourses and spiritual retreats may be enough motives to begin the day. The idea is to find what inspires and moves you. With that inspiring motive, when you give the thought of rising early to your subconscious mind before sleeping, you are more likely to remember that motive as soon as you open your eyes in the morning. This will make it easier for you to spring out of bed. But if you don't have a compelling reason for getting up, you will keep snoozing the alarms and make it hard for yourself.

Me: So, with a rock solid reason I can program myself to jump out of bed every morning all chipper and happy? That sounds too good to be true!

CONVERSATION 7

Success: It really works, try it. Then you can also visualize yourself getting up and finishing all your work cheerfully and thereby avoid getting stuck in the web of lazy thoughts. On the other hand, if you haven't given any motive to your subconscious mind, and have spent time worrying, surfing the internet, chatting, or watching TV before going to bed, then you won't be able to recall any reason to leave the bed in the morning. In such a case, lethargy will grip you and you will keep lying in the bed wondering, "Why do I need to get up now?!"

This behavior is completely opposite to what is experienced during meditation. When you sit for meditation, the tendency of your body keeps you from sitting quietly. Your mind starts searching for reasons to stop the meditation and get up. You may remember chores you need to carry out or any of a thousand other seemingly important things. Any external noise could interrupt you and make you abandon your meditation right then. This usually happens on a subconscious level, without you being aware of it. You don't even realize when you got the thought and when you got up. You could avoid this by simply giving an intention to your subconscious mind, such as: "I will practice meditation for minimum 10 minutes even if I remember any urgent task."

So, what's the message? *Whether you begin meditation or go to bed, it's very important to have an intention.*

Me: Wow, it's like I've been programming myself without realizing it! When I plan something with my friends that requires leaving early in the morning, I go to sleep with those thoughts, and those thoughts make me wake up early and I have loads of energy while getting ready. Usually I'm up even before the alarm rings!

Success: Yes, everyone experiences this one time or the other. You just need to give your subconscious some reason to pop out of bed and it will serve you.

✺ ✺ ✺

ROCK SOLID REASONS TO MAKE WAKING UP AN EASY JOB:

1. To be more productive

An important reason to wake up early is to be more productive. Those extra morning hours will give a good beginning to your day. The wonderful feeling of waking up and diving straight into action is an added bonus.

You can experience it only if you do it. Then again, you have to be motivated by something that is valuable to you. You can use this time to build some skills and to acquire some knowledge to assure your success.

There's no better way to start the day than with a small achievement of getting up on time that gives you a sense of completion and fires you up for the rest of the day.

2. To be self-disciplined

If you want to be successful, you have to bridge this gap between your goal and accomplishment. Remember, discipline is the bridge between goal and accomplishment. And to enjoy a disciplined life, you need to wake up on time. You can see this discipline in all successful people's lives. You cannot afford to waste your morning hours like this by lying in bed for no reason.

Discipline can be built and strengthened by taking up small challenges, conquering them, and then gradually moving ahead to bigger ones. It's like progressive weight lifting.

Try this for developing the discipline of waking up on time: Initially, get up say 15 minutes earlier than your usual time for a week. Then extend it to a fortnight, and then to 30 days, to seal in the habit. After that, you'll be so habituated to waking up early that you'll find it hard to sleep in.

3. To make your day smooth-sailing

Those who wake up on time are relaxed throughout the day. Studies show that such people experience lesser levels of stress as they complete their work on time with ease.

4. To be healthy

The body's 'circadian rhythm' (the biological clock) is a physiological cycle, which is adapted to the 24-hour day. When you rise with the sun, your biological clock becomes attuned with the rhythm of nature. Sleeping and waking up at the same time every day makes you healthier and helps to set the sleep-wake pattern in this circadian rhythm. Decide what time you want to get up each morning. This will be the time your eyes automatically open most days of the week. Setting your alarm for that time every day will help set your circadian rhythm for that time.

5. To attain your ultimate purpose

If you know the ultimate purpose of your life, you won't have any problem getting up on time. The ultimate purpose of every human being is to realize and get established in the original state of Self, and to express the qualities of the Self such as unconditional love for everyone, joy, peace, creativity, courage, patience and other beautiful qualities. If you remember your higher aim, you will never want to sleep in.

However, many people decide new goals for themselves but fail to remember them. This happens because either they soon forget about it or are not passionate enough about it to follow through. If you are wrestling with this kind of situation, ask questions, instead of suffering. Ask yourself: What is my ultimate purpose? What is my final aim? If I succeed in achieving this aim, what would be its impact on me, on other people and on the world?

Use these questions to jumpstart your contemplation before going to bed, and the understanding you subsequently gain will help you jump out of bed early in the morning!

THE 5,6,7 THINGS
TO ENJOY GETTING UP ON TIME

If you have set what you will do before hitting the sack and as soon as you wake up in the morning, your life is set! Hence, try these 5, 6, 7 things.

5 STARS BEFORE BED

Any one or all of the following five activities at bedtime will aid you to leave the bed early in the morning. Hence give yourself 5 stars before bed:

GIVE YOURSELF A MOTIVE

You can then recollect that motive as soon as you awaken, which will help you to get out of bed. Set your weekly or daily motives. E.g.: If I get up early, I can make time to pursue my hobby.

PICTURE THE DAY AHEAD

Think of all the things you are going to do the next day. Start with the moment you wake up and go through the whole day. E.g.: I am going to wake up at 6 a.m. tomorrow and then at 6:30 I will...

SET A LOUD ALARM

Keep the alarm nearby. You can also choose a radio or an MP3 player with an alarm function.

DRINK WATER

Drink a big glass of water before going to sleep. You will probably have to visit the washroom early in the morning because of that.

RELAX

Before going to bed, take a warm bath, read a book or listen to soft music. These will help you to get a good night's sleep and complete your sleep cycle. This in turn will help you to get up refreshed and on time.

SUPER 6 SHOOTERS

Use these super 6 shooters once the alarm rings in the morning, so that you instead of hitting the snooze button, you shoot out of bed.

1. Throw off the covers
2. Turn on the light
3. Drink water
4. Pump yourself up with music
5. Stretch your body

The moment you wake up, recollect your ultimate aim. Your ambition to achieve your aim will pull you out of sleep.

A challenge a day keeps sleep away. Thus, take up a daily challenge that will compel you to leap out of bed each morning.

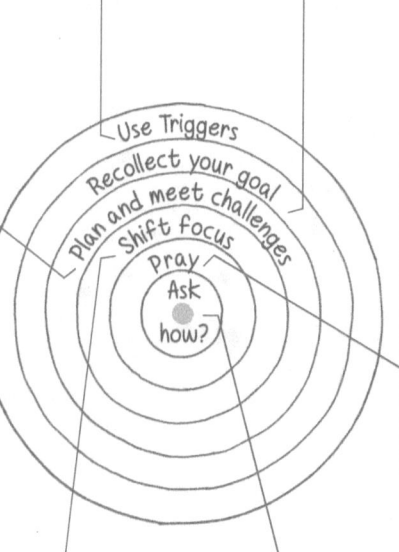

Use Triggers
Recollect your goal
Plan and meet challenges
Shift focus
Pray
Ask how?

Start your day by offering a heartfelt prayer to the Almighty. "Thank you God for this beautiful day."

Shift your focus to the larger picture and see the domino effect caused by the simple act of waking up on time. Imagine how you would feel when you will finish all your tasks on time. This will make you jolt out of bed.

Instead of falling prey to thoughts of laziness, ask, "How can I jump out of bed now?" It will help you to find the most suitable technique to pull you out of bed.

007 COMMITMENT BOND

> These 7 commitments will help you spring out of bed. Hence, make this commitment bond with yourself.

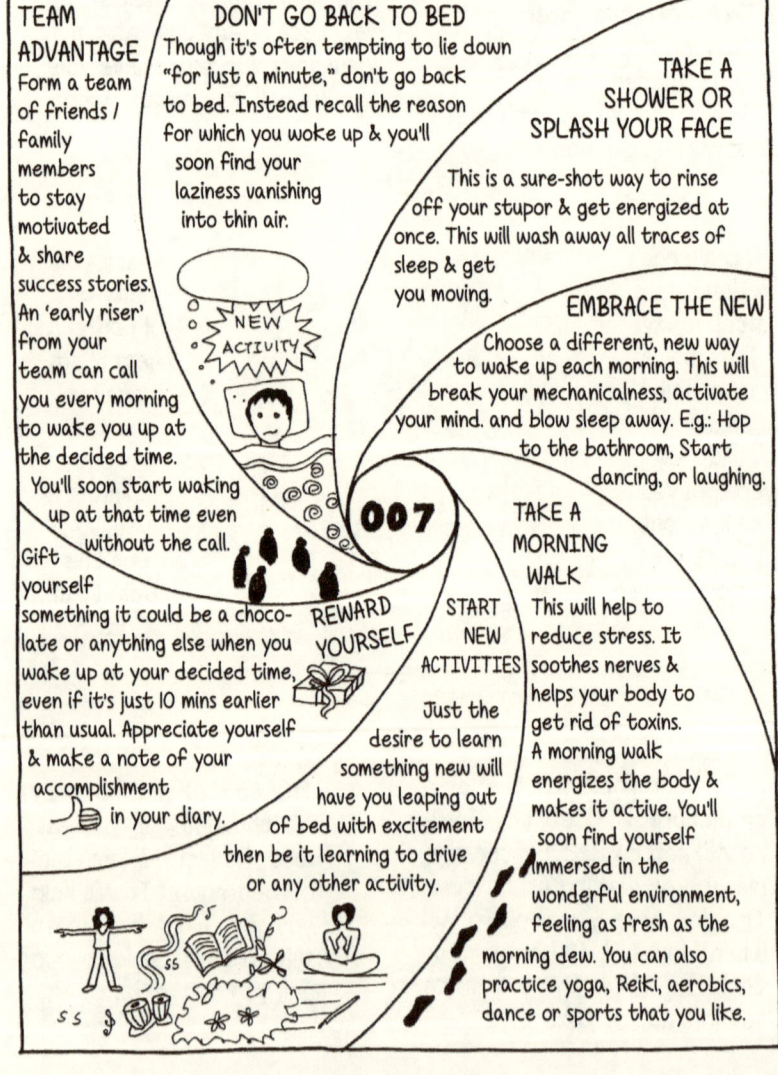

TEAM ADVANTAGE
Form a team of friends / family members to stay motivated & share success stories. An 'early riser' from your team can call you every morning to wake you up at the decided time. You'll soon start waking up at that time even without the call.

DON'T GO BACK TO BED
Though it's often tempting to lie down "for just a minute," don't go back to bed. Instead recall the reason for which you woke up & you'll soon find your laziness vanishing into thin air.

TAKE A SHOWER OR SPLASH YOUR FACE
This is a sure-shot way to rinse off your stupor & get energized at once. This will wash away all traces of sleep & get you moving.

EMBRACE THE NEW
Choose a different, new way to wake up each morning. This will break your mechanicalness, activate your mind, and blow sleep away. E.g.: Hop to the bathroom, Start dancing, or laughing.

REWARD YOURSELF
Gift yourself something it could be a chocolate or anything else when you wake up at your decided time, even if it's just 10 mins earlier than usual. Appreciate yourself & make a note of your accomplishment in your diary.

START NEW ACTIVITIES
Just the desire to learn something new will have you leaping out of bed with excitement then be it learning to drive or any other activity.

TAKE A MORNING WALK
This will help to reduce stress. It soothes nerves & helps your body to get rid of toxins. A morning walk energizes the body & makes it active. You'll soon find yourself immersed in the wonderful environment, feeling as fresh as the morning dew. You can also practice yoga, Reiki, aerobics, dance or sports that you like.

QUOTES

I'd be more frightened by not using WhatEver ABILITIES I'd been GIVEN. I'd be more frightened by PROCRASTINATION & LAZINESS.

~ Denzel Washington ~

Nobody can think STRAIGHT who does not work. IDLENESS warps the MIND.

~ Henry Ford ~

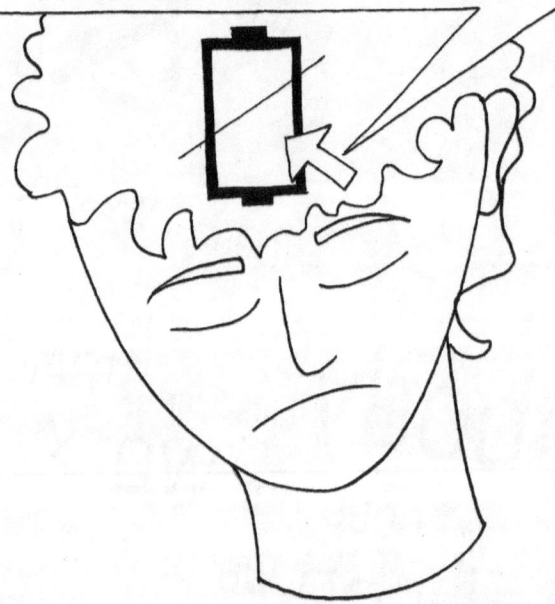

CONVERSATION 8

Me: Hello Sucess!

Success: Hello to you too. So, what should we discuss today?

Me: Well, I want to tell you that I get the theory, but I have some questions. What about the situation where it's NOT wrong if you don't do a particular task. Like my mother asks me to go to the market and I say I can't because I'm completely wiped out. That doesn't mean I'm lazy, right? She always seems to ask me to do stuff when I'm exhausted!

Success: Ok, let's consider a similar example. Suppose a man has just returned home from work. As soon as he walks in, his wife asks him to go to the market and pick up something. However, he has already been to the market on his way back from the office. Hence he starts shouting, "I was just there! Everybody was in a mad rush and the shopkeepers are rude. I have already bought all this stuff you told me in the morning. No way am I going out again! Why don't you understand that I am completely drained? It's simply beyond my capacity!"

What do you think when you hear someone say that something is beyond his/her capacity?

Me: Well, I totally understand how he feels! Going to the market again is the last thing he wants to do.

Success: Ok, but you missed the point. The fact is he doesn't know his capacity. Just by saying, "I'm incapable of doing this," a person reduces his capacity to almost nothing. This is an example of exaggeration. Instead of just saying, "It is beyond my capacity," one should honestly ask, "If this is beyond my capacity, then what exactly is in my capacity? Am I aware of my potential?"

Me: Yeah, but when I'm really tired and I think I can't do it…"

Success: These are your thoughts, but is it the truth? Take a minute. Rethink on it and check it out for yourself. Visualize yourself in a similar situation where you are completely tired.

Me: Well, I guess it's not the truth. There goes that excuse! This is because even if I've had an exhausting day, many a time I turn into a superman when we friends happen to plan a party for the evening.

Success: You nailed it! "Going out again is simply beyond my capacity"—this statement by the man in that situation makes it seem like his wife had asked him to jump across the sea!

NO LAZY PHILOSOPHY PLEASE!

It's better to be lazy than waste your time getting tired.

Me: And wrestle sharks if he should fall in!

Success: The man's exaggeration—that going to the market again was beyond his capacity—indicates his limited thinking. Uttering such words repeatedly can hammer them into one's psyche.

This is the problem with human beings. A person thinks something and says it, and then he begins to believe it as the truth. Only an honest individual or an evolved person without an ego can save himself from falling into this vicious cycle.

Me: What does ego have to do with it?

Success: Suppose the man from the example is told, "Actually it is within your capacity. You can go to the market even in this condition." If he has a strong ego, he will be furious. "How can you say it's possible when I have said I can't do it?!" But if he thinks about it honestly, a new perspective will open up. Instead of saying "no" straightaway, he will ask himself, "Is it really impossible for me to return to the market? Or, when I said it was beyond my capacity, did I exaggerate it in such a manner that I felt it was the truth?" Therefore, be wary of the words that come out of your mouth. Otherwise, just like a spider, you may get caught in the web of your own words. Always ask yourself, "Is this really impossible?"

Me: As they say: Impossible = I M possible. So, do you want to say that the man should go to the market?

Success: I am not implying that the man should definitely go to the market. Don't get into the details thinking about whether he went to the market or not. Instead try to grasp the meaning of his words and their impact on his behavior. Understand how he has created a wrong habit of exaggeration for himself. Think about your own capacity and whether you are stifling it with your own words. This is a very important aspect, which people tend to ignore.

Me: Hmm... I do exaggerate sometimes. We all do. Let

me tell you the most common exaggerations. "I can't live without her or He's good for nothing or I always screw up…" Actually, they don't mean anything! They are all exaggerations!!

Success: Exactly. When you exaggerate and announce that something is "impossible," you close yourself off from every possibility of success.

Me: Whoa! That means exaggeration is dangerous.

Success: Absolutely! Therefore, always allow new possibilities to open and do not shut them off.

You have a lot of powers. You have unlimited potential, even if you haven't ever gauged how enormous that potential could be. When you realize the extent of your potential, you will understand how many things, which you had previously thought impossible, were actually within your reach. To achieve this potential and in order to use it to create something magnificent on this planet, you must get rid of these wrong attitudes. Many new creations haven't come into this world, just because of this habit of exaggeration, which is why one needs to work on getting rid of it right away.

Once you start working on overcoming this habit, you may find yourself accomplishing some tasks, while you may be unable to accomplish certain other tasks. But if you proclaim outright that something is beyond your capacity, then you don't even try it. You lock out every possibility of success. Therefore, practice being open to possibilities. This will help you to keep your options open for a bright future. Believe me, you really have enormous capacity.

Me: Sometimes it's not easy to believe that I have enormous capacity.

Success: Well, why don't you check it out for yourself?

Whenever you hear yourself say, "This is impossible," or, "This is beyond my capacity," ask yourself if this is the truth or merely an exaggeration. And be honest while answering it. You'll find that most of the time, it's an exaggeration. An honest answer will automatically shift you to a higher level of confidence. **HONESTY IS THE KEY.**

If you keep exaggerating to yourself, saying, "This is impossible," or "This is beyond my capacity," you will start believing it. This thought then becomes a belief and strengthens the indolence in your body. In reality, most problems do not exist anywhere but in your own thoughts.

Me: Yeah, my imagination scares me sometimes!

Success: That's because thoughts impact you in a big way. You have to break away from the mind's habit of exaggerating things. Otherwise, you tend to seal even a single negative thought that enters your mind, i.e. you believe that thought to be the truth. When you are free from this habit, you act like an envelope which is open from both the ends. Thereby, in any situation, you won't stamp on any thought passing through the envelope of your mind to be the truth. You allow it to slip away from the other end of the envelope. You don't make your own stories regarding the event. In short, if you don't exaggerate, it stays small and insignificant.

Not only is a lazy person always exaggerating things, he often does not know that he is doing it. You may think, "This is beyond my capacity," and stamp on it, and then you actually start believing it. If you catch yourself doing this, ask, "What picture am I creating in my mind, based on this event? Am I making more of this than I need to?" Let's say you just told yourself, "I am completely drained." Is that true? No!

Me: I get it. If I were completely drained, I'd be asleep, or dead!

Success: Exactly! When you think that you're totally drained, tell yourself, "I have an enormous reservoir of energy inside me." When you keep repeating the truth that you have enormous capacity, you will start believing it even during situations that seem difficult.

Me: So my number one task is to stop exaggerating, right?

Success: Correct.

Me: I should talk to myself so that I come to believe: Everything is possible unless I tell myself it's impossible. "Nothing is made in this world which is beyond human capacity to achieve," as they say. That means I should change all my limiting thoughts and embrace new ones. As a result, my response will change from negative to positive. I will find myself losing the habit of exaggerating and welcoming all wonderful possibilities awaiting me.

Success: You're getting smarter by the day! ☺

TAP INTO YOUR HIDDEN ENERGY RESERVES

How often you stayed up studying all night before your exam, and yet went ahead and got through it with flying colors?! How did this happen? The energy needed for such intense study was already within you. Exam tension brought out your hidden reserve.

However, in general scenarios, where you don't have exam pressure or any other pressure, you work for a while and then feel tired and so you stop working. What most people don't realize is that all human beings have three levels of energy within them. Most often, they stop working as soon as they exhaust the first level of energy. However, if they push through and keep working for a little longer, they start accessing the second level. Some people call this their "second wind." Here's a rundown of the different levels of energy.

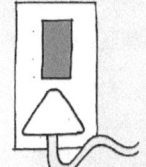

- First level energy: The energy that your body uses to perform routine tasks.

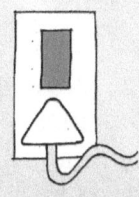

- Second level energy: The energy reserve that surfaces when you need to do a little more than your usual routine—like a special occasion, festivals, trekking or exams—anything that is not a part of your daily routine. Whenever you use more energy than usual, you are tapping into the second level.

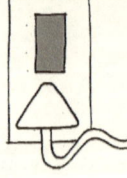

- Third level energy: This deepest level of energy reserves is usually used only in times of emergencies. But do remember that you have this third level of energy and keep using it intermittently. Here is a wonderful example of a girl using the third level of energy.

Mahika, an eight-and-a-half year old girl, was chosen for the coveted Bharat Award for saving the life of her four year old brother, during the Uttarakhand floods in 2013. On 16th June 2013, Mahika was in Kedarnath valley with her family and relatives. At around 7 P.M., when she was alone in the hotel room with her younger brother, floodwaters slammed into the building. Lights went out and the room was filled with water and debris. Mahika saw her younger brother being swept away in the floodwaters. Without knowing how to swim, braving the debris coming her way, she pulled her brother out and stayed in the room for 3 days without any food or water, holding her brother. The braveheart, when asked how she did it, says, "I don't know from where I got the strength. I just knew I had to save my brother and put all my energy to hold him close to me."

(http://mief.in/mahika-gupta-a-true-braveheart/), (http://indianexpress.com/article/india/india-others/9-year-old-delhi-girl-saves-brother-at-kedarnath-gets-bravery-award/)

This story is a tragic one and yet inspiring at the same time. If an eight-and-a-half year old can tap the third level of energy, so can you. All it takes is will.

Whenever you feel like you need to stop working due to exhaustion, remind yourself that your body has the energy to do wonders. Remember that nature has already inserted abundant powers in your body; you simply have to keep reminding yourself about them and use them.

QUOTES

Nothing is difficult;
it is only we
who are indolent.
~ Benjamin Haydon ~

If you want to become
trustworthy,
never give an excuse that
there is no time
because you have as
much time a day
as a successful person has.
~ Sirshree ~

Me: Good morning, Success!

Success: Good morning! So, was yesterday's discussion useful for you?

Me: Definitely. After learning about exaggeration, can I get some advice on one more scenario from my life?

Success: Sure.

Me: Whenever I ask my younger brother to do some stuff for me, he comes up with reasons such as: "I have to finish my homework." Of course, my parents agree with him and he doesn't do what I asked him to. So, I get mad at him. On the other hand, when someone asks me to do something for them, I too don't want to do it because I have some other stuff to do.

Success: I got it. Close your eyes for a moment.

Me: Off to imagination land, are we?

Success: Kind of. Imagination is where you decide what's possible. So, come on, close your eyes and ask yourself, "Do I ask myself the right questions in such situations?" Don't open your eyes immediately. Just ask this question to yourself.

Me: (Closing eyes) Why would I ask any question to myself in such situations? I don't have time to quiz myself on stuff when I'm just trying to get through the day! I don't think I need any questions here.

Success: I'll get to that in a moment. But right now, continue with this exercise. You might already be asking some questions in such situations. Dig inside. Find out what kind of questions do you usually get. You can open your eyes when you get the answer.

Me: OK. There are some questions that I am tempted to immediately throw to anyone who asks me to do something; questions like: "Why do you ask me to do stuff at this time?" Or, "Can't you do it yourself?" Or, "Why don't you understand that I too have a lot of things to do?" But I guess these are not the right questions; are they?

Success: I'm afraid not. Because these won't help you to liberate yourself from sloth. Asking the right question is an important step in getting rid of this attitude.

So, you were saying that when you ask your brother to do some chore for you, he starts giving excuses under the pretext of homework. Indirectly, he says how the task cannot be done. In this situation, people may think he is right, and that he cannot possibly do that chore because his priority is school. If he does not do his homework, he will get poor grades.

NO LAZY PHILOSOPHY PLEASE!

Hence, people are likely to tell him not to worry about doing you a favor.

But, supposing your brother had asked himself, "How can I do this chore and still complete my homework?" Then he might have started thinking about solutions such as: "Could

I do it after coming back from school? Can I wake up just a few minutes earlier to do this?" and so on.

Me: This implies that just asking the right question can open up options and help find a solution to a problem.

Success: Spot on! Let's elaborate on this. For instance, you suggest a new idea for designing a creative cover for your college magazine. But before even thinking about it, the graphic designer says, "No! This idea cannot be executed. It simply cannot be done."

Me: Oh! So, this answer is from his habit of exaggeration?

Success: Yes. He is exaggerating that the idea cannot be executed. He may think of himself as an expert, but his answer proves that he is still an amateur. This is because an expert never gets trapped in the thinking that something is impossible.

When a disciple tells his spiritual master, "This task cannot be done," the master will say, "There are ten ways of doing this job. You just need to find one." If the disciple is still unable to find a way to carry out the task, the master guides him and says, "Since you need training, you will not be given the solutions directly. You will not progress if you are spoon-fed. Hence, you need to first investigate by yourself. Solutions manifest automatically on investigation."

Getting back to the expert, an expert doesn't rely on just one solution but instead starts thinking about all the different solutions that could work. This habit always keeps him on the path of success.

Me: He starts thinking outside his own box!

Success: And that's the secret, isn't it? We have all got so used to the word "impossible," that whenever we come across a task that is outside our comfort zone, our mind immediately declares: "Impossible! This cannot be done."

Me: But as you said, the truth is that nothing is impossible and one just needs a slight shift in thinking to make things possible. I guess this is where the role of asking the right question comes into the picture.

Success: Correct. If you are directly told a solution, you are likely to resist it. That's human psychology. But there is no resistance if the answer comes from within you. To receive answers from within, you need to learn the art of asking the right questions. Get used to listening to your inner "yes"— your intuition.

Me: Yeah, I don't always listen to guidance from anybody, including my inner self. Is it really that important?

Success: Absolutely! If you want to make your life easier and smoother, if you have a higher aim in life, and if you truly want to create something awesome on this planet, then it is crucial to listen to your inner voice.

All you need to do is ask a question with a little twist.

Instead of saying, "This work cannot be done," ask, "How can it be done?" With this question, you release your resistance and allow the guidance to flow from within—from the Self. Even a single thought of "impossible" can impede the flow from the Self. In reality, the flow from the Self is strong and it can offer minimum ten solutions to every single problem you encounter. However, if right at the start you say, "It's impossible," then how can things proceed? Therefore, it's important to develop the habit of receiving guidance from within—from the Self, which is the source of everything. And always say "yes" to the guidance coming from the Self.

Asking the right questions will make you see a lot of things. I don't mean to give you more homework, but you will grow by leaps and bounds in any area if you write down what your answers, insights and inspirations are. When you bring an idea into writing, you are likely to gain even more insight. It all depends on how much importance you give to the process of seeking answers. Giving attention to something will help you receive more of it, while you will stop receiving things you do not respond to/give attention to.

You have to be ready for certain wisdom; otherwise it won't make sense to you. Once you're ready, the floodgates open and you become more receptive.

So, if you ask the right questions, such as, "How can I accomplish this seemingly impossible task?" and allow the answers to appear, you would begin to receive the solutions to your problems.

Me: With this habit of asking the right question, I too won't have the word "impossible" in my dictionary just like successful people!

Success: That's possible! 😁 The great wonders that you see in this world are just because of the word "possible." Some people said it's impossible to build a certain bridge because of huge mountains. While some others said, "It is possible," and built a gigantic bridge. This is how monuments are created. It is such monuments that hold a place in history. They were created only because some determined people believed that it was possible. However, these people did not develop confidence all of a sudden. It was a continuous process and the result of persistent work. So the moral is:

EVEN SEEMINGLY IMPOSSIBLE TASKS CAN BE ACCOMPLISHED SUCCESSFULLY WITH PERSISTENT PRACTICE.

It is during such persistent practice that one may come across an "Aha!" moment. And these people are the ones who go on to perform deeds for which the world remembers them.

Me: Oh! So it all boils down to one word then: "Possible"? And the people who use the word "possible" go on to create great things, while the people who use the word "impossible" only sit and watch!

Success: Yes. People who believe in "possible" are receptive for guidance from the higher realms. For the higher beings, the Earth and the other realms are not separate; in fact these beings are always transmitting ideas to create something new on Earth. But someone here should be ready for receiving those ideas and implementing them.

Me: Wow! I feel like the sky opened up and all this wisdom is showering on me. I want to be one of those people who say "possible" to everything.

Success: Wonderful! Then be open to coincidences, synchronicity, flashes of insight, gut feelings, intuition or the inner voice. You'll initially want to pick the most obvious cues, and then, slowly, you will also tune onto the subtler ones. This guidance will give you confident direction—and presto, no more laziness! Because you would want to work on it.

Suppose two songs are being played simultaneously, one at a higher volume than the other coming from a distance. If asked to listen to the lower volume song, a lazy person will say, "No. I will first listen to the song that can be heard loud and clear." This is because it will require less effort. However, a person who wants to get trained to listen to even subtle sounds or guidance from the Self—i.e. someone who wants to learn the art of seeing the wonders that manifest from the invisible realm—will make an effort to hear the song that's coming from a distance. He will train himself by asking the right questions.

Therefore, when you say you don't want to do some work, it's not about the work you avoid by making excuses. Rather, it's about the habit of making excuses that blocks the natural flow of guidance from the Self, which can bring you success.

Me: Hmm... So, first I need to stop exaggerating. Secondly, instead of being unhappy when faced with a seemingly impossible task or a distressing situation. I should hit the PAUSE button and ask myself the right question. That way I'll find solutions and be motivated to do something about it.

Success: Here you go! I'm glad you got this!

Me: You are making it easy for me to imagine being someone who can create something new, something life changing.

Success: That's the way to fly to success. It's what you've wanted to know all along, isn't it?

Me: Fly to success! I like that. On my own private jet!

Success: Great!

Apart from the questions we talked about, there is one profound question which is the ultimate tool to free yourself from laziness. We will talk about it in our further conversations.

Me: I can hardly wait!

※ ※ ※

CONVERSATION 9

One may say, "I have so many limitations; how can I achieve success?!" The truth is that limitations force you to think in a new and creative manner. They force you to improvise and innovate. Therefore, consider limitations to be wings with which you can fly to success. However, this requires knowledge about your true potential, faith on nature or God, as well as confidence and courage to implement this guidance in life.

Thus, whenever you are in the grip of lethargy or your body experiences the limiting force of inertia, use this mantra and ask yourself, "Can I do this task despite my lethargy?" (You know the most probable answer!) With an honest answer you will embrace the word "possible" even if lethargy tries to grip you.

At the next step, you need to clearly communicate to nature what you are in favor of: lethargy or enthusiasm? Hence, when you verbalize either aloud or in your mind, "Though I feel lethargic at this moment, I am in favor of activeness, I am in favor of enthusiasm," you start receiving energy from nature. You get what you ask for. This is the law of nature. With this, soon your flight will take off from the planning stage towards success.

So, in this action plan, identify a task in your life that appears impossible to you, and ask yourself, "How can this be accomplished despite my lethargy?" Write down 10 ways to carry out that task.

For example, someday you wake up in the morning and think, "I really cannot go to the gym today. I was up late last night, hence I need to rest now." In this situation, ask yourself, "How can I go to the gym despite my lethargy?" You can get 10 solutions, such as:

1. I can go to the gym now and rest after coming back.
2. I can go along with my friends in order to feel motivated.
3. I can take a hot water bath, feel refreshed and then go for the workout.
4. I can go to the gym a little late today instead of missing it altogether.
5. I can have a glass of juice to energize myself and then hit the gym.
6. I can boost up my energy by giving suggestions to my body like: "I am energetic and active now."
7. I can ask myself the right question: "Is going to the gym now really impossible?"
8. I can put on some music and feel energetic.
9. I can go to the gym in the evening.
10. I can _____ .

The task that I find impossible to perform:
_____
_____

How can I do it despite my lethargy?
1. _____
2. _____
3. _____
4. _____
5. _____
6. _____
7. _____
8. _____
9. _____
10. _____

QUOTES

Between the great things we cannot do and small things we will not do,
The danger is that we shall do nothing.
~ Adolff Monod ~

CONVERSATION 10

Me: Hey, good morning Success! Yesterday it was an interesting discussion on exaggeration, excuses and asking the right questions. By exaggerating we are in a way just giving another excuse to duck out of our responsibilities. This has been a real eye-opener.

Success: Perfecto!

Me: I now see that I tend to put off some tasks. But there is a reason. Some tasks are just so boring that I don't even want to touch them. How do I deal with these, because when I look at someone as successful as Richard Branson or Amitabh Bachchan, I don't think they would ever procrastinate their tasks… they are so committed to their work! I too want to be like successful people who are free from the habit of procrastination.

Success: So, you have actually answered your question.

Me: How ?!

Success: Here's your answer. If procrastination stops you, then commitment will save you. Laziness and commitment are opposites. Lazy people who do not commit to the task will never complete it. But if you commit to a task, you break the pattern of laziness and get out of the habit of procrastination.

Me: I never thought of commitment as a habit.

Success: Yes, it's a habit which will always keep you on the path of success and prevent you from getting diverted from your goal.

Some people keep boring tasks on the back burner and focus only on their favorite activities. Although they appear to be very active, they are simply unable to accomplish the boring tasks. They keep trying to dawdle and wriggle out of those tasks, often without realizing it. Now that sets a perfect platform to welcome procrastination in life.

Let's look at commitment from a different perspective. Suppose you have planned an event in your college and you are looking for someone who will help you with the execution of this event. What kind of person would you like to work with? You have two options: 1) A friend who likes to anchor public events but does not like to carry out the related groundwork such as listing and studying the participants, or dealing with logistical issues. 2) Someone who is committed to make the event successful and hence is ready to execute every task that comes up to make the event a grand success.

Me: This goes unsaid. None of us would ever want to work with a person who is not committed. We all want committed people around us... Oops! So, when people look towards me, they too would expect me to be committed!

Success: That's it!

Me: Hmm... I wish people would always want me to be around them. This means I really need to be committed. It's all about my attitude.

Success: Bravo! So, all in all, finding something boring is an attitude, isn't it? Anything is only as boring as you make it.

EVERYBODY LOVES A COMMITTED PERSON

Me: Aha! So, if I am committed to a goal, I won't find any task that is related to it to be boring. My entire focus will be on achieving the goal.

Success: Exactly. You remember we spoke about the ultimate aim of human life, i.e. experiencing and expressing the Self through one's body. The more you are committed to this aim, the closer you will be to achieving this aim. Hence, to enable the expression of the Self through your body, you will tend to develop the habit of performing any and all tasks, even unpleasant ones, with a good attitude. Just don't think of them as unpleasant, think of them as "okay" if not outright fun. If you can do that, you are moving in the right direction. Otherwise, even one wrong habit can hamper the expression of the Self.

Me: Ok. But I don't find daily chores interesting. How does commitment to a higher aim help me with that? Can I make my daily chores fun?

Success: Yes! Here's what you can do. When you are faced with a task you dislike, remind yourself: "This task is an opportunity to train my mind." And it's always easy for the Self to express through a body which has a trained mind. That is how the Self can create something new, something divine on Earth. Tell yourself, "I am committed to this task and I will find the best way to address it." Once you develop this habit, you will realize that no work is as boring as it first appears. On the contrary, you will get insights on how it can be made interesting. You will find many new ways to carry out the same chore creatively every day. The more you strive to become creative, the more fun you experience while performing these chores. Additionally, finishing the chores will also save you from the guilt associated with avoiding them.

Me: That feels good. However, I have a big list of the activities that I don't like.

Success: And in the future too, you'll come across many such activities that you may not like at all—at work or at home. This is where your practice of performing boring tasks pays off and you can easily complete the activities that you don't like, without resistance or stress.

Me: Wow! Is that really possible?

Success: When you experiment with this, you will see it for yourself. Not only that, but as you free yourself from lethargy and rise higher, you'll feel that this could happen so easily only because of the Self's divine grace. It's the Self within you or your inner voice that reminds you about your higher aim and therefore everything happens effortlessly. People normally do not recognize this divine grace and hence grumble about every small task that they have to do.

In fact, these very tasks are the opportunities to learn something new every day and prepare yourself for the highest expression of the Self through you. Nature is constantly giving you these opportunities. When a new project arrives, a person who is running away from work that he detests, says, "I don't want to do this." Yet, when he is forced by circumstances to do it, he does it. And on accomplishing it, he thinks, "I'm glad I tried it. Otherwise, I would never have realized that it's actually kind of interesting." Once you delve into the project, you'll begin to notice its various facets and you will realize that it's not as difficult or boring as you first assumed it to be. But for that you'll need to recognize the opportunity and begin that work.

Me: Like they say, "Eat the frog first." Do the thing you don't want to do first and then everything after that is super easy!

Success: Right.

Me: I feel like I'll very soon be free from this pattern of laziness and will evolve into the attributeless state needed for the expression of Self. A new ME! Full of life!

Success: You shall see what you believe. But there is much more to it.

Me: What's that?!

Success: Moving ahead, this journey will not only take you closer to the attributeless state, but will also shift you towards impersonal or selfless work.

Me: Impersonal or selfless work? Do you think someone like me can do something like that when I'm already struggling to just get through my daily routine?

Success: Why not? In fact, when you start implementing the knowledge that you are receiving, you will find that selfless work is automatically happening through you. When you implement this wisdom, you give the opportunity to the Self to work in your life.

You will then start experiencing the unlimited joy of impersonal or selfless work or work that is done for the benefit of all including you. When you develop a taste for impersonal work, even the most boring activities get done with ease. You may not like every task that needs to be done for impersonal work. In fact, there may be many you don't like. However, since they're for the greater good and you have love for impersonal work, you manage to complete those tasks smoothly. That's how you develop the habit of commitment.

Have you seen people who were so immersed in working for their impersonal goal, that they forgot the world around them? What was it that made them achieve the impossible?

Me: Yes, I've seen some inspirational movies based on the lives of such great people! They are always immersed in their work so passionately; I really admire them. One can easily feel the fire burning inside them to do something for humanity. I really wonder where all that energy comes from.

Success: It comes from the divine joy of doing impersonal work or serving others. Later they move on to become great scientists, social workers, writers, artists, remarkable film makers, inventors, etc.

Me: Now I know how they achieve those heights. They never find any activity boring or difficult. In fact, they are so committed that they could easily manage to do each and every task related to their goal. It's like they developed a superpower just for this one thing.

Success: Very true. On the other hand, the one who thinks only on a personal level has limited thinking. And it is this limited thinking that gives birth to words such as "impossible". Just hearing about a new task or a seemingly boring task creates panic and uneasiness in such kind of people. This keeps success at bay.

Therefore, see how you can develop a selfless attitude to lead an impersonal life. This will help you to overcome the habit of avoiding boring jobs.

Me: Do you mean that I should volunteer for an activity based on a noble cause?

Success: That could be one of the options. However, you can also link your day-to-day activities to a higher, noble purpose. If you are planning to be a successful businessman, contemplate on what kind of products or services can elevate the consciousness level of people or bring transformation in people's lives. Every day, before you start working on any project, ask yourself, "What difference can I make to the world through this project?" And then transfer this vision to each and every employee of your company.

If you cannot immediately start something bigger, think what is the best you can do for a smaller group of people at present? For example, you can discover some good learning techniques which you can share with all your classmates that would help them with their challenges. You could think of creating such a platform that will allow students of all types to participate freely and bring out the hidden talents in them. Think out of the box.

Me: Wow! That sounds exciting. I always wanted to do something different, but never actually tried. Now I will surely go ahead. At least I'll work on some ideas that will help me and my classmates to develop some skills or enhance the subject knowledge to get through those job interviews.

Success: Fantastic! This shall help you to develop an impersonal attitude. Now that you've made up your mind, let me give you some quick tips. Bring them into your daily routine and you'll see enormous energy flowing in your body to create something amazing.

Me: I'm already feeling that energy in my body!

Success: That's the power of an impersonal aim! 😃

Okay. Here is the first tip: Don't wait to be in the "zone"!

Many people wait to be in a particular mood or to get into the "feeling to do it" before beginning a task. Instead of starting at once, they wait to be "in the zone." However, if you begin a task and do it for some time, you'll find that you automatically slip into the "zone." This happens because your actions are actually controlled by your willingness to do them. However, interest levels and the "feeling" to do something are not in your direct control. So, instead of waiting for them to strike, why not induce them by just getting to work? The next time you take up a task, tell yourself that you like to do it, and watch how fast you manage to complete it! In this way, you can fulfill all your commitments.

Me: But what should I do when I'm wrestling with my thoughts and can't stay motivated?

Success: This problem has a simple solution. Start working faster.

Me: Are you kidding me? How is stepping on the gas going to motivate me?

Success: I am serious. Try this at least once and see for yourself.

Start working faster instead of waiting for the right mood.

For example, walk quickly, write quickly, dial the phone number quickly, take a bath quickly, clean your table quickly, and so on. This increased speed will prevent the mind from getting moody. An individual is unsuccessful if he depends on his mood to start working. What if your mother had waited for the right mood to start cooking when you were a little kid? How often would you've gotten any food at home?

Me: Man, I never knew such spiritual stuff was actually so practical!

Success: Well, of course it is! It's meant to give you the ultimate experience of your true nature! So, now you understand the importance of being liberated from slavery to mood. A committed person is capable of beginning work on a project at any time, instead of waiting to be in the mood, and will complete the project on time.

Me: That's fabulous!

Success: I agree. Now let's move ahead.

The second tip is:

Ask yourself every night, "Is there anything more I can do before going to sleep?"

You may be surprised to learn that many successful people once avoided work like the plague. However, they received guidance and started working on getting rid of that wasteful habit and now follow a much improved lifestyle. Each night, they ask themselves, "Is there anything more I can do before going to sleep?" Usually, they will find some small task that needs to be done, and they do it. This enables them to stay ahead of their schedules and go to bed with a feeling of satisfaction.

Me: This habit will help me to be committed for developing a new and useful habit of being committed ☺.

Success: Wise interpretation! Now, let's get to the third practice, which is called:

"A little, but today."

If you want to take on big projects, then break them down into smaller pieces and work on one piece at a time. The mind will make excuses when given something big. But, however big a responsibility or project, it can be accomplished when taken up in small chunks. Hence, do a little, but do it today. This is a key secret to success.

If you want to be free from laziness, then begin today.

If you cannot wake up one hour early, then wake up 5 minutes early, but start today. If you want to read a book, read a chapter or even a page, but do it today.

Along with this technique, always remember this powerful statement:

EVEN IF ONE PERSON IN THE WORLD CAN DO A PARTICULAR THING, THEN YOU CAN DO IT TOO.

Once you are committed to accomplish a job, then don't look back and keep moving ahead.

Me: One step at a time! OK. I won't wait to be in the "zone." I will ask myself before going to bed, "Is there anything more I can do before going to bed?" and I'll tell myself, "A little, but today." That doesn't seem very difficult. Who knew discipline could be so easy?

Success: Imagine the habit of lethargy as a thick wall. A conscious effort to daily practice the techniques I've shared with you is like pounding a hammer into that wall. It may not seem effective at once, but if you continue doing it, you will notice that small cracks have started appearing. The longer you pound on the wall, the larger the cracks get, and eventually, the wall collapses. Thus, if you consciously practice these techniques, you'll be left with only as much inertia as you need to function optimally.

Me: Wow! That's exactly what I want. Thank you so much.

Success: You are welcome!

MY SCOREBOARD

Tick those areas where you tend to procrastinate and make them possible

BORING TASKS	MISSION POSSIBLE						
WEEKLY SCORE BOARD	M	T	W	T	F	S	S
Organizing my room/wardrobe							
Repairing broken items							
Washing dishes and cleaning the kitchen							
Writing a diary or reading a book							
Completing homework or projects							
Joining a class related to my passion							
Paying bills							
Developing a positive habit							
"Boring" tasks like renewing a library book or auto registration							
Spiritual practice (meditation, prayer, listening to discourses, etc.)							
Activities that require following up with others							
Avoiding confrontation							
Exercising every day							

Don't wait to be in the "zone"!

Also, make a list of activities you have been running away from and tackle them first. Take the three small steps you've learnt today and apply them consistently. You'll see amazing results in that area, which will trickle over to the other areas too! Then the boring tasks will no longer seem to be boring, and all your activities will give you joy.

QUOTES

Every choice you make has an end result

~ Zig Ziglar ~

It is our choices that show what we truly are, far more than our abilities.

~ J. K. Rowling ~

WHAT IS YOUR HIGHEST CHOICE

FOR THIS LIFE AS WELL AS

FOR THE AFTERLIFE?

CONVERSATION 11

Me: Good morning, Success!

Success: A very good morning to you too!

Me: The tips you shared yesterday are really powerful. They leave no scope for the mind to wriggle out of any kind of work or give any excuses. With this, I have another question for you. Every self-help stuff talks about making the right choices: *You are what you choose; you are what you think,* and so on. Could making a right choice also be a step in overcoming laziness?

Success: Yes, definitely! I must say your contemplation on shedding laziness is showing you many solutions.

Me: I guess so! :)

Success: He who makes the highest choices always finds ways to accomplish any goal. Making the right choice will take you closer to your goal. Let's understand...

Me: Wait, wait, wait. See, I made the highest choice of getting rid of laziness so that I can create something wonderful on this planet. And this is how I found this new solution, i.e. making the highest choice.

Success: Brilliant. Now let's dive a little deeper in your question as you

have found one more way to shed lethargy. By now you must have realized what activities you habitually avoid. Is it joining a gym or getting some stuff from the grocery store that your mother asks you?

Me: You're hurting me now! You know I avoid both of those activities. 😫

Success: 😄 Then ask yourself right away, "What's the highest choice: to shirk or to do it now?" Your answer to this question will help you to complete that activity. If you cannot make the highest choice due to external circumstances or any other reason, go for the second-highest choice.

Me: Second-highest choice? What could that be?

Success: It could be finishing a part of the activity if you cannot complete the entire job at that moment. Or doing some groundwork related to the task in advance. But it should never be the lower choice, i.e. putting off the job. For example, enquire about the gym, its timings, fees, etc.

Me: A little but today!

Success: Correct. You also have to practice this step in routine life. If you're feeling hungry, your highest choice would be to nourish yourself with fruits, vegetables or any other healthy food. However, if it's difficult to get those at that moment, your second- highest choice should be food items with minimal fats but it should never be junk food. This will protect you from inertia. However, remember that your aim should always be the highest choice.

Me: Yes, yes. I am what I eat! I remember you said junk food increases inertia.

Success: Good. This habit of going for the highest or second-highest choice has a deep impact on your life. It will always prevent you from making lower choices.

Additionally, cultivating this habit of asking yourself whether you're making the highest choice in every situation will help solve many problems. All you need to do is remember the right solution at the right time. But many people don't remember the right solution in times of stress.

Me: Why is that?

Success: The answer is very simple: they have not practiced the solution; they have not worked on the habit of remembering solutions in times of need. When they face any problem, their focus is on the problem or its repercussions and not on the solution. That is how they can't remember the solution though they have many remedies. Hence, they cannot take the necessary steps. Then, suddenly, a solution springs to their mind and they apply it, which solves their problem.

Me: So, what you're saying is that if I want the right solutions at the right time without worrying about it, I have to make a habit of remembering them. But how do I make a habit of remembering all the solutions that you have been teaching me?

Success: Making anything a habit is very simple. It's all about programming your mind. To understand this deeply, yet keeping it simple, let's say the mind is divided into two: conscious mind and subconscious mind. The workings of the conscious mind are visible, while that of the subconscious are invisible, yet powerful. The conscious mind is like the captain of the ship, while the subconscious mind is like the engine room below. The subconscious mind works according to the instructions received from the conscious mind. The subconscious cannot distinguish between right and wrong. It is a faithful servant—honest, trustworthy and it never disagrees with anything you decide. It only executes and manifests the thoughts provided by your conscious mind into reality.

Me: That means I have to program my subconscious mind by giving instructions using the conscious mind.

Success: That's right. And the mantra is repetition.

PROGRAMMING = REPETITION

When something is done repeatedly, the subconscious mind takes it as a signal that you want to make this a habit and starts doing it automatically, so that you don't have to consciously remember it again and again. It doesn't think whether it's a bad habit or a good habit.

Me: That sounds like I pull up a computer program to solve a problem and actually I'm the one who programmed the computer.

Success: Yes. That's a good analogy. The main reason behind a person's inability to get rid of lethargy is that once the conscious mind gets trained to act in a particular manner, then the subconscious mind gets programmed to react in the same manner. If the subconscious has been programmed for lethargy, then the individual always tries to find a way that involves the least amount of movement or activity. It's the same tendency that makes him say, "It's okay if I do this work tomorrow." This habit of procrastination becomes a major cause of failure in his life.

Me: Considering that the subconscious mind turns all repetitive thoughts or actions into habits, I feel it's all the more important to be aware of our thoughts and actions!

Success: Absolutely. THEREFORE, TO BEGIN WITH, PROGRAM YOUR SUBCONSCIOUS MIND BY THINKING CONSCIOUSLY IN THE RIGHT DIRECTION—TOWARDS YOUR ULTIMATE AIM—AND FEEL PASSIONATELY ABOUT IT.

Me: Right. So, if my first reaction is "no" for any new task, then I should practice asking the right question: "How can it be done?" If I practice this consciously and consistently with every task I undertake, soon I'll develop a good habit.

Success: Yes, because this will positively program your subconscious mind. You will then see how your initial thought of "no" is cancelled by a resounding "yes". You will no longer have to think whether a task will be accomplished or not. Even if you do, your subconscious mind will give you the correct solution and remind you to ask the right question. As a result, you will ask, "Am I exaggerating when I'm saying that this cannot be done?"

In this way, you'll find that only those thoughts will arise in you that have reached the subconscious mind through repeated practice.

Me: I now understand the importance of contemplation. I can clearly see how much I had fallen into the trap of wrong habits in order to protect my lethargy.

Success: Splendid indeed! Only a person who contemplates honestly can realize this. Honesty is an important quality. It helps you to understand the patterns of your body and to grow spiritually.

Me: You know, I have started developing interest in spirituality. I always believed it to be boring and something that one may practice after retirement. But now everything sounds so easy and simple with spirituality.

Success: Spirituality is all about the Supreme Truth and of course it's simple and interesting. It's just your wrong assumptions that keep you away from it. It's extremely essential to listen to the Truth so as to make the subconscious aware of the importance of Truth. You need to repeatedly perform certain spiritual actions, such as reading and listening to the Truth, contemplation on the Truth, rendering service for the Truth, devotion and spiritual practice (sadhana) in order to fully absorb the Truth. Truth seekers need to cultivate these habits if they want to attain the Truth.

In fact, you should examine every little choice you make. If a person makes the highest choices in this life, he will do the same in his afterlife too. Whatever thoughts a person harbors during his death, it is likely that he'll begin his journey into the afterlife with the same thoughts. He'll be able to give priority to higher choices over comforts and conveniences.

However, in order to recall this wisdom on his deathbed, he needs to have practiced it consistently during his lifetime. Only then it is possible to practice it in the afterlife too.

Me: Whoa! Those are serious implications! So, it means that carrying out spiritual actions which you mentioned is the highest choice that I should make in this life.

Success: Absolutely. It is the highest choice and it will help you make the highest choice in every situation, even in the face of difficulties. Your subconscious will always respond with a "yes."

If you can already choose between the good and the bad, then you will learn to choose between good and better. This will help you to choose the better option, even in small things. After constant practice, you will eventually be able to choose between better and the best.

For example, a person comes across various items while shopping. He may like everything he sees. In such cases, only the one who has practiced will be able to make the right choice. Otherwise, people are unable to make better choices and end up spending much more than what is actually required. Mental lethargy does not allow an individual to think. He will pick anything that comes to him and without thinking he says, "Yes, this is fine. Let's go for this."

The moral of the story is, if you want everything to be the best in your life, you need to free yourself from physical as well as mental lethargy.

Me: Isn't it mental lethargy that grips us and prevents us from thinking what the right choice is?

Success: Yes. I will give you an example. A person is at a multiplex theatre and has to choose between two movies. One is better than the other according to the box office, but he has already watched the better one. At this point, he just wants to spend his time watching some movie, so he has to pick one of the two. What would an untrained mind choose?

Me:

Success: He's likely to watch the same movie that he has already seen, simply because he has assumed it is the better of the two. But what's the point? What can he achieve with this choice? Even if the other movie is not as good as the first, it can still teach him something new. Even a flop movie can have a good message. When you watch such movies, you sometimes wonder, "What a great message! Who said it's a dud? It's a good movie... It wouldn't have flopped if the presentation was better."

Me: I've experienced this.

Success: Only those who are serious about learning and creating the habit of making the highest choices can make the right choice. Otherwise, one chooses the same old options and remains blind to their consequences. Many people ignorantly choose to repeat their past. Hence nothing new can enter their lives. Their choices belong to the lower level or, at the most, average.

When you make the highest choice, you become aware. Your thinking expands and you can take the right decisions. Later you will congratulate yourself for making the highest choice.

In the multiplex example, if the person watches the second movie—the one he has not watched before—he will realize that he has made the right choice at the right time. He will also realize that nothing could've been achieved by watching the same old movie again, unless it's a great inspirational movie. He would've experienced the same things he did the first time around. He would have waited to watch scenes that he had already watched. He would've thought, "I liked that dialogue," and would have sat waiting for it to appear.

Me:

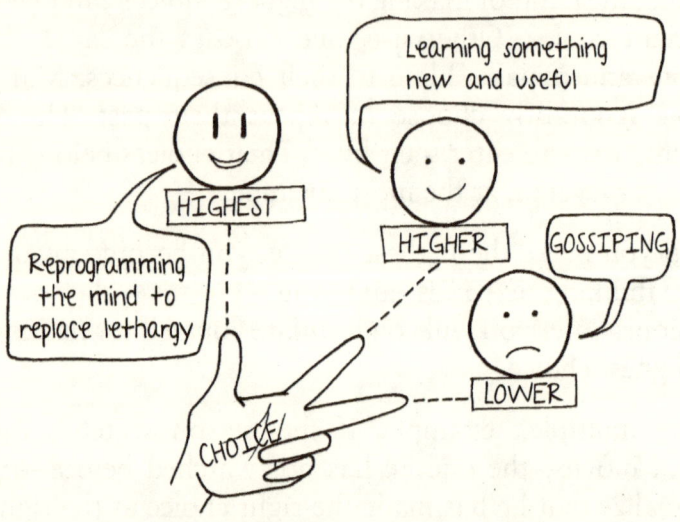

Success: Making new choices is an important step to take in your life. That's why I'm asking you to practice choosing the highest option so that you can rise up from your present level of thinking. You may not always succeed in making the highest choice, but there are infinite possibilities. When you choose the new and the unknown, you become capable to face the consequences arising from it.

Me: I have already made the highest choice of doing impersonal work. Now I choose to program myself for activeness.

Success: Fabulous!

✺✺✺

BREAK THE BACK- BRIDGE

Obstacles in decision-making as well as in making the highest choice are what cause you to put off tasks. As long as you can backtrack, you will continue to doubt your choices and avoid doing things. But, when you take a firm decision, you burn your back-bridge or escape route. You will not have any option but to move ahead, because there is no path to go back. This gives the benefit of a "do or die" situation, with no chance of running away from your decisions.

For example, if a student wants to top his class or college, he must announce this intention to his friends or family. Once he's announced a decision like this, everyone who heard him will keep inquiring about his preparation. These reminders will inspire him to work harder to achieve his goal. Thus, by announcing his intention, he has effectively blown up the escape route behind him.

Therefore, take up the responsibility of completing all your tasks, of keeping your commitments and of breaking the back-bridge.

QUOTES

The difference between average people and achieving people is their perception of and response to failure.
~ John C. Maxwell ~

If the doors of perception were cleansed, everything would appear to man as it is, infinite.
~ William Blake ~

CONVERSATION 12

Me: Good morning, Success! Today, let me ask you about my friend Devansh. He's a bright guy. He was not at all lazy and topped his class most of the times in school, but now in his college days he seems very passive and does not strive for success anymore. He seems disturbed many a time and success eludes him. Doesn't he want to enjoy success anymore? Has he had enough of it?

Success: It's not that way at all. Everybody wants to enjoy success at every stage of life, no matter what goal they have set for themselves. The only problem is they have burdened themselves with false notions and beliefs.

Me: What kind of false notions and beliefs?

Success: Let's understand this gradually. There are some beliefs you might be familiar with, such as: "I should always be perfect," "I should not look dumb in front of others," "People should find

If you are late, don't go.

NO LAZY PHILOSOPHY PLEASE !

me intelligent every time" and "Everyone should like me." These are mostly wrong beliefs and notions.

Me: Why, what's wrong with those? I don't agree that those are wrong beliefs. We all want to look good in front of others and strive for perfection. I mean, we're always told to do our best, right?

Success: Of course, you always have to do your best in order to achieve the best. That's a good habit. However, the problem arises when one starts thinking obsessively about it. Because that creates stress, then stress overwhelms them, which in turn leads to stasis. This means they are unable to do anything. Thus, whenever such type of people need to begin any work, these wrong beliefs pop up. For instance, when a student is considered very intelligent because he scores well, he starts linking his value to his scores. He feels that people around him would look down upon him if he fails to score well even once. Whenever he tries to prepare himself for exams, he finds himself trapped in this cycle of stress. This is how he has created illusions about himself, which then leads to unnecessary stress, which in turn results in delays and inadequacy in his work.

Me: Yeah, there are some students in each class who have no life because they're always behind wanting to score more and more, and if they get anything less than a perfect grade, they fall apart!

Success: Their false perception makes them unable to enjoy studies as well as the beauty of life. Let's see what may have happened with Devansh. Initially, in school, he was not under any pressure to perform and his studies were going well. Now he feels forced to study because of the perception that he has created for himself, which is: "I'm worthy of getting a good job offer only if my grades are perfect." As soon as this wrong belief comes into play, he starts believing that others would consider him unworthy if he does not score well, and feels pressurized to study. This pressure takes all the pleasure out of his studies and his mind starts wandering in these self-made stories. He becomes more and more preoccupied with living up to people's expectations. He constantly thinks, "What will people say if my scores are low?" or "What would happen to my image?"

Me: Oh, so this is how he got stuck in these false perceptions and unrealistic expectations!

Success: Yes. And that could be the reason behind his disturbed state of mind. He's not lazy but the pressure of having to live up to unrealistic expectations leaves him stressed and unable to perform his activities efficiently. His illusions regarding his image have instilled the fear of failure in him. As a result, he may keep away from trying new things or even doing his usual work. That is why you find him inactive.

Me: You're right! This year Devansh is afraid of losing face due to a low score. So, nowadays he thinks, "What if I haven't prepared enough? Maybe I should stay back this year, study more, and then appear for exams next year."

Success: It's the stress and fear caused by his self-image that makes him find excuses to avoid exams. When a person thinks that multiple tasks need to be finished simultaneously and perfectly, he gets trapped in those thoughts. His energy gets drained due to this anxiety and he cannot perform those tasks in a proper manner. It is particularly important for such people to remind themselves to stay away from false notions. If they don't do that, they will realize too late that the situation that had them in a tizzy was not such a big deal after all. It was only a story that they had created. Now you know how Devansh's perceptions and illusions have become obstacles in his success.

Me: Yes! That's an alarming situation. Some people create such beliefs and impose them on others, which then become a part of everyone's belief system. Even if we don't want such beliefs, it's due to the influence of people around us that we unconsciously adopt those beliefs.

Success: Yes, that's what happens. However, you can safeguard yourself from this problem by applying nature's Law of Influence, which states that:

"PEOPLE CANNOT INFLUENCE YOUR THOUGHTS UNLESS YOU ALLOW THEM TO."

Knowing this law, whenever you find people around you carrying wrong beliefs and creating illusions for themselves and also for others—directly or indirectly—be aware to not allow their thinking to influence you. Tell yourself clearly, "I don't need to buy into these wrong ideas; I can easily give my best by applying the wisdom I have gained through these conversations and that is how I allow my higher self to express itself. When I am free from false notions, the best will manifest by itself."

Understanding this, check whether similar beliefs are making you inactive, despite not naturally being so. Does your work suffer due to stress? If you fail to finish your work despite being active, ask yourself, "Have I fallen prey to any illusions? Are my fears paralyzing me?"

Me: Again, I need to ask the right questions.

Success: That's right. Questions have the power to alter your wrong thinking and give you the right direction.

Also, a person may take longer to complete some work in an attempt to achieve perfection. He feels that the extra time he's taking will help him find a method or solution that will make his work better. However, very often, that does not happen; instead his work gets delayed more and more. And ironically, the more he tries, the worse the quality of his work gets. And because he is so focussed on "not failing", he subconsciously invites failure.

Me: Why is that?

Success: That's because of a universal law, called as the Law of Focus, that states: "WHATEVER YOU FOCUS ON WILL GROW IN YOUR LIFE." Hence, focus on what you want, not on what you don't want. If you want success, focus on success. Do not say or think along the lines of: "What if my work is not good? I don't want to fail. What if I fail?" This means you are focussing on failure; and hence failure will manifest in your life.

Me: Whoa! This is very important indeed. I'll have to watch closely as to what I am focussing on in every aspect of my life.

Success: Absolutely!

Me: We were earlier discussing about wrong beliefs and stress. You know, my uncle leads a team in his organization and is always stressed due to delays in his work. And he is always saying, "People put their trust in me. So, now I have to follow through. They will not trust me if I fail to accomplish every single task that is expected of me." More the responsibility, more is the illusion.

Success: That's a perfect example. The leader is always stressed due to his perceptions about himself and his team. If he realizes that one can perform very well even without this stress, he would not have been stuck in these illusions.

When people face "do or die" situations or some special situations, they manage to accomplish even so-called impossible feats. This gives them confidence, and then they say, "Oh! I did this so easily! And I needlessly thought it was impossible because I was entangled in some big illusions."

Me: But there are many situations in which one becomes anxious on thinking even a little about the result or the process of the task.

Success: In such situations when a task seems stressful, the individual should ask himself, "Can I perform this task bit by bit?" Then he should assure himself by saying, "I simply have to keep performing my job to the best of my abilities, using the best resources available to me at this time. Results will automatically be taken care of."

This means he should do whatever is possible for him, without being overly worried about the results. Eventually, he will realize that he has achieved much more than he had believed possible. That's how you often hear people saying, "I didn't think I could do so much! The results are much more than I had expected." Consequently, their confidence gets a boost. Hence, you should keep doing all that you possibly can. Very soon, you will be surprised with the accumulated results. Just remember: *One step at a time.* Take the first step with this understanding and the rest will follow automatically.

Me: And that's where one stumbles!

Success: 😃 Don't worry, it's easy to deal with this. Let me tell you about a student who used to goof off in class and evade his studies. Homework and study were the biggest challenges of his life. He just couldn't get down to doing his homework, no matter how much time he had, and just the thought of studies would put him off. Once, his teacher gave all the students a period off, basically a whole hour to do whatever they pleased. This student was baffled as to what to do for that one hour, since his friend with whom he used to spend his time was absent that day. So, he opened his book thinking that he can at least see what homework he's got today and then he started doing his homework as he had nothing else to do. To his great surprise, he finished his homework well within the hour.

He then thought to himself, "Oh! This got done so easily! Why did I think it was hard?" Thus, the boy who was always wriggling out of studies learned his lesson through one simple incident. This usually happens in every student's life.

Me: I know, things are not as difficult as we imagine them to be. But I guess we wait for certain incidents to happen to learn a lesson.

Success: But you don't need to wait for incidents to teach you. The solution is: Begin your work much before any wrong perceptions take root in your mind. Do a part of the work in your free time, however small you can manage, rather than wasting that time. With this, you will find that many of your tasks are getting completed in this manner. You will also figure out that tasks that seemed impossible were not actually all that difficult. Thus, whenever you find anything difficult, make it simple by dividing it and do it a little at a time.

Me: I think this will really make everything easy. Remembering the example of the student, I can always motivate myself to take the first step.

Success: Great! So, to put it in a nutshell, wrong perceptions lead one towards stasis. When a person feels stressed even before beginning a task, he's stressed not because of the task, but because of the stories he has created in his mind about the task. This makes him so anxious that he feels paralyzed and can't work as much as he would have otherwise under normal circumstances. Due to this, success evades him.

Therefore, the solution is "a little at a time."

Me: Got it! Henceforth, no stories, only 'doing a little at a time.' You are a genius, man!

※ ※ ※

CONVERSATION 12

Most successful people have the habit of writing a diary. They often write down their goals, tasks and thoughts. As another universal law says: BEFORE ANYTHING IS CREATED IN THE PHYSICAL PLANE, IT IS FIRST CREATED IN THE MENTAL PLANE. Therefore, when you write a diary, you are creating mentally by consciously thinking about what goals you want to achieve. This will help you achieve those goals and manifest what you want in life. You could benefit a lot by doing this regularly. Here are some ways to maintain your diary:

• Goals and Tasks
• Write down your goals and tasks in your diary, calendar, computer or cell phone. Remind yourself of your higher aim of life and be prepared to train your mind.
• Then with the feeling of happiness and faith, give suggestions to your mind: "I am complete, and through this completeness, all my work is completed on time."
• Make a list of your tasks and resolutions which will lead you towards your goal.
• Prioritize each task according to its importance and urgency.
• Give each task a deadline and make sure to complete them on time.

- Visit your task list every day before going to bed. And tick mark the tasks which you could accomplish on that day.
- Check if you can complete the remaining tasks on the same day, and if not, at least finish a part of those.

This will give you the feeling of completion. Those who do not value this quality will not maintain a diary and are likely to forget some tasks. This tool of writing down tasks is very effective and is useful in breaking the habit of procrastination or forgetfulness.

Completing any work on time proves your dependability. The inspiration you gain from each success makes you remember even the smallest task. As a result, people will see you as a reliable person and extend their whole-hearted support to you.

- Thoughts

You can also note down the thoughts, merits and demerits that you find in yourself while working on a task or project, and use those to improve yourself in the future. Also write down the feedback you receive from others and prepare your action plan based on self-analysis and the feedback. All of this will help you to focus on how to handle the responsibility you have been handed in the best manner. Take full advantage of such opportunities without being afraid of present responsibilities. This will break the old tendency of working unhappily and you will start working with joy and a smile.

Also, reflect upon the stories you create about the goals you wish to accomplish. The fear of what people will say has killed more dreams than anything else in the world.

Write down all the false perceptions that create stress in your mind and lead to inactivity. This will keep you aware every time you take up a new project.

QUOTES

> We are all pencils in the hand of God.
> ~Mother Teresa~

> Knowing others is wisdom, knowing yourself is enlightenment.
> ~ Lao Tzu ~

CONVERSATION 13

Success: Hello, Ankit! What are you thinking?

Me: I'm thinking that whatever you have said about various laziness patterns, the bottom line is that they have all formed due to our own mental attitude. The solutions you have shared so far are helping me in a big way to free myself from the clutch of lethargy. I feel active and energetic to do anything and everything. I just cannot imagine how awful my life would have been had I continued to be lazy... yuck!

Success: Great! This realization is very important. This will keep you on the right track. Soon, you will see me manifesting in your life.

Me: I am so excited to experience how success feels! Do you have some magical power that can help me to break free from these lethargic patterns all at once? Now I want to feel alive every moment and allow the Self to experience life through my body.

Success: I was waiting for this 😝! I feel that you are now ready to receive the ultimate wisdom.

Me: Oh!! Am I?

Success: Yes. Okay, tell me when you drive a car, do you ever say, "I am this car"?

Me: Now you're just messing with me. I'm seriously looking for that ultimate insight. And let me tell you that no sane person on this planet would ever say that!

Success: Right. So, you say, "This is my car."

Me: Of course, I say, "This is my car."

Success: Fine. What about that shirt then; do you ever say that the shirt you wear is you?

Me: Oh, come on! Whether it's a shirt or a car, you know the answer does not change.

Success: Okay, regarding your hand, what do you say: "This is my hand" or "I am this hand"?

Me: Will you please stop asking me such silly questions? It's my hand. I am not the hand. And if you are going to ask me the same thing about all my body parts, then the answer will be the same for any part of my body!

Success: 😄 I'm trying to drive home the point that anything with which you use the word 'my' or 'mine' cannot be 'you'.

Me: I know that! I say, "This is my hand... I cut my finger... I hurt my hand," and so on. Why would I say, "I am the hand"? How can I be the hand, when I am the entire body?

Success: Wait. Answer this last question. If you want a good physique, what would you say, "I want to build my body" or "I want to build myself"?

Me: I would naturally say, "I want to build my body."

Success: So, when you say "my hand," you cannot be the hand. Similarly, when you say "my body," can you be the body?

Me: No... in a way, no... I mean yes... now you lost me!

Success: Here is the insight you need to deeply contemplate on: You are not the body.

Me: How can I not be my body?! I cannot accept that.

Success: You're finding it difficult to accept because the belief that you are the body has taken deep roots within you. You never realize that all your thinking and doing is governed by this limiting belief that you are the body. Now you need to imbibe this ultimate truth that you are not the body.

When you yourself said that you cannot be any particular body part, then would it be correct to say, "I am the body"? What is the body after all? It's nothing but an assortment of all your body parts.

Me: Whoa! I kind of understand it, and I don't.

Success: This is because your head says that it's logically correct. Let's carry out an experiment. Close your eyes and follow the instructions that I am going to give you to understand this experientially. This exercise will help you to experience the truth that you are not the body.

Me: Okay, I am ready.

Success: Good, so let's begin. Relax your body. Take a deep breath. Be calm. With eyes closed, take your attention to one of your hands. Ask yourself, "Am I this hand?" You don't have to answer immediately. Just rest with the feeling of what is being experienced.

Now take your attention to your legs and ask yourself, "Am

I these legs?" The answer may come as: No.

Then move on to your ears, eyes, nose, mouth, and slowly shift to your entire face. Ask yourself, "Am I this face?"

Likewise, take your attention to each body part one by one and ask whether you are those parts.

Now go within and mentally observe your internal organs.

Ask yourself if you are the lungs, heart, liver, kidney, stomach, and so on.

Now shift your attention to all your body parts collectively and hence your body.

Continue being in the feeling of what is being experienced for a while.

Now, slowly open your eyes. Tell me, what did you experience?

Me: (after a period of silence) Well, that was incredible!

As I was observing each body part, I began to relate to what you were telling me earlier. I experience this body. I can observe this body. I'm not really the body since I can observe it, right? Now I can understand our first conversation in the true sense, and also I have read that the body is my vehicle or just a medium to experience and express myself on Earth.

Success: That's perfect! You are not the body. When you start experiencing this truth, you will understand that you are actually separate from your physical body.

Some people lose their limbs in accidents. Yet they never say, "I am incomplete now, earlier I was complete." The experience within feels complete. This is because when your body is cut, you do not get cut. When you start experiencing this truth, then the root of all false beliefs—

"I am this body"—will break.

In this way, you will know your true self. You will experience your true self and attain real happiness. At the same time, your attachment to your body will begin to dissolve.

Me: I think I'm realizing what you've been saying. I am full of life. That's my real nature; not lethargy, which is a pattern of the body. I guess that is exactly what I am experiencing right now.

Success: Perfect. Now, let us carry out another experiment that will help you to dive deeper in this experience of who you truly are.

Here is the profound question that you should always ask yourself: "Who Am I?"

Me: "Who am I?" You know, I do get this question many a time. But I don't know the answer. So, I don't pay much attention to it.

Success: Many people get this question but very few try to find the answer. Rest of them engage themselves in the mundane. Only those, who consistently try to seek the answer, understand the deeper aspects of life. Then life becomes blissful for them.

"Who Am I?" is such a profound question that constantly asking it will help you realize the answer. No other question or mantra has as much power to open up the channel for the Self. Even if a person does not have an answer to this question in the beginning, understanding will dawn if he keeps repeating the question time and again.

Me: So, actually, who am I? I want to ask you the same question. Surely you know?

Success: You don't need to ask me, you need to ask yourself. The answer cannot be told in words, it can only be experienced. I can only show you the path to the answer.

The journey is yours. To know who you actually are, you need to contemplate upon who you are not. Such as:

"I am not this body" because when I say "this is my body," then it is 'my,' it is not 'I'.

"I am not my five senses. And I am not my nose, ears, eyes, tongue, or skin because I use these sensory organs."

"I am not the breath due to which this body-mind is functioning. I am not the mind or the intellect, which thinks about what I should be."

If you are not all of that, then what is left that you can be? Only YOU are left! It's you who possesses this body. It's you who is the master of your intellect. It's you who is the silent witness of your mind.

Me: That's amazing!

Success: Yes. You are amazing. To experience the depth of the answers coming from the Self, repetition of the question "who am I?" is important. There are some things the Self wants to express. But since you don't pay attention to those things or you are not receptive to them, they are suppressed. Repeatedly remembering and asking for them triggers and allows them to come forth. With this, the truth unravels that you are not the body, you are just using this body for your life on Earth. Therefore, when I say you cannot be lazy, I am pointing to the real you and not the body.

Me: This knowledge is surreal. Who would have thought that I am not the body?!

Success: ☺ This knowledge about one's true nature acts like a bomb for lethargic people. The more your conviction grows on this truth, the more will lethargy be unable to overpower you. If you believe that you are the body, you'll always think, "I want more rest," "I want all comforts and conveniences," "I should keep all work aside and take more care of myself" or "I don't have any more capacity." Hence, fully absorb this supreme truth: You are not the body. This is the ultimate understanding to liberate yourself from indolence. If you do not use this understanding, you are making your body ill.

Me: Really? Was I making my body ill till date?

Success: Yes. It happens so gradually that an individual doesn't realize until it takes form of a disease. As you know, a machine will rust and not function properly if kept idle for a long time. It needs to be operated at regular intervals, so that it can work for many years. An unused machine deteriorates, and when it's time to use it, it causes damage instead of working optimally. Likewise, your body is a machine. You need to keep it active in order to maintain it functionality.

Me: To do that, I have to free my body from excess lethargy.

Success: Precisely. You will use the understanding "I am not the body" more as you begin to shift towards a higher state of consciousness. Understand that your body is a machine and make the best use of it. It is an instrument and must be treated as such.

If you have been using a computer throughout the day or using too many applications simultaneously, it "hangs". It stops working. It is better to shut it down for some time and then restart it. Likewise, your body should be given adequate rest at night. If you understand that the body is a machine, you will give it adequate rest, but only as much as is required to re-energize it. On the other hand, if you do not have this understanding, you will give excessive rest to it, you will continue to be in your comfort zone for a longer time, night or day, inviting many diseases.

Me: Particularly during winters when I don't want to leave my warm and cozy bed at all.

Success: That's a common occurrence everywhere. But as we discussed, that is not true rest. It is indolence. Until you begin to see yourself as separate from your body, you will continue to fulfill its craving for comfort and conveniences. That is excess lethargy, which needs to be banished from the body. Hence, whenever you are hit by lethargy, remind yourself that you are not the body. Ask yourself what you are protecting. Ask whether, by not using it, you are helping your body or hampering it.

This understanding will help you to detach yourself from the mistaken belief that you are the body. It will help you to connect to your true self.

Your body is the medium or instrument for expressing your real self. This instrument is meant to serve you, hence you need to operate it properly. Scissors maintain their sharpness only with regular use. A sharp axe will cut down more trees in a shorter time than a blunt axe. Thus, as you use your body, you are sharpening it and increasing its efficiency with balanced exercise and rest. If a lethargic person truly understands that he is not the body, he will never live in sloth again, not even by mistake.

Me: It means I will never live in sloth again!

Success: That's exactly what I want.

✸ ✸ ✸

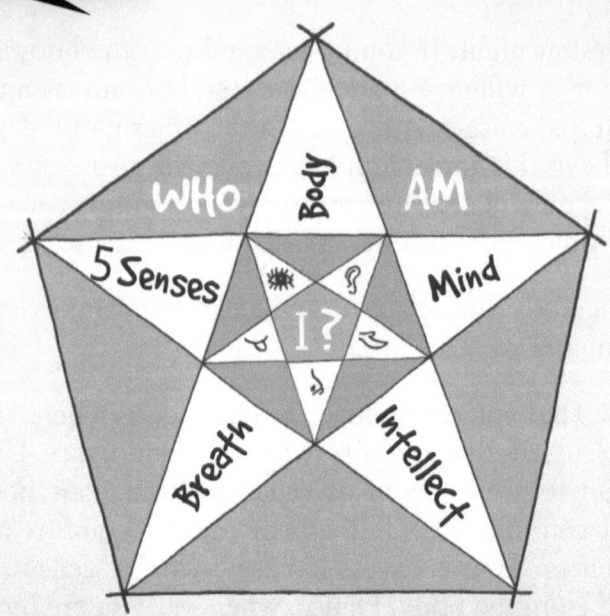

BE IN THE STATE OF WHO YOU ARE

Let's practice the following meditation to build the conviction that you are not the body.

1. Sit in a comfortable position so that there is no tension in any part of your body.

2. While sitting, ensure that your spine is straight, and makes a 90 degree angle with the ground. This helps you to sit in meditation for a longer duration.

3. Now start watching your thoughts. Thoughts are nothing but triggers. For example, if a thought is of the past, it takes you down the memory lane. "If only" thoughts—if only I get this... if only this happens... if only I were...— lead to fantasies and daydreams. Do not identify yourself with these thoughts. Look at them as distinct entities, separate

from you, and you will not get drawn into them. Let them come and go; do not go behind them.

4. Look at thoughts as if they are stickers that stick to your body for some time. They are temporary. Every now and then, a new sticker gets stuck on your body and after a while it falls off. (You can also look at your emotions and sensations in a similar manner.) See lethargy as a temporary sticker that is stuck to your body. Merely watching it as a sticker will help it to fall off.

This understanding will help you maintain a state of detachment in spite of various distractions and lethargy won't be able to overpower you. You will thus be able to remain in the experience of your true self.

5. When a person sits quietly at one place for meditation, indolence invades the mind and leads to daydreams. Thus, lazy people are likely to daydream during meditation. If this happens with you, remind yourself that meditation is not meant for that and bring yourself back to the present. You have to find various ways to do this, since the mind is likely to cling to indolence.

6. If various thoughts arise during meditation and try to entangle you, remind yourself that these are mere stickers and come back to experiencing the true Self. Simply witness any thought that comes up—with detachment. This is called Thought Watching Meditation.

7. Make meditation a part of your daily routine. If you can do this, you will automatically progress towards the attributeless state and get established in the state of bliss. Everything in your life will then happen smoothly and beautifully.

QUOTES

❝ Devotion is that supreme gift after the achievement of which one rarely aspires for anything else. ❞

~ Sirshree ~

❝ Bottom line, your body is a temple, and you have to treat it that way. That's how God designed it. ❞

~ Ray Lewis ~

CONVERSATION 14

Me: Hello, Success! I am deeply moved. Remembering the truth that "I am not the body" makes me feel light. It is the most beautiful experience I've ever had. Now I want to be in this experience for the rest of my life.

Success: That's great! It's due to divine grace that you are experiencing it. Be thankful to God for this experience. And pray to Him that you want to be in this experience for the rest of your life; as very few are able to live in this experience.

Me: I shall pray to God every day, as well as thank Him for blessing me with this higher wisdom and beautiful experience.

Success: Your prayer will certainly be fulfilled because prayer has immense power. It is the ultimate tool to receive what you want. And if you have faith, then your prayer becomes even more powerful. With faith, everything is possible.

Further, try to bring the understanding of "I am not the body" in your practical life. Don't limit your identity to the outline of your body. Don't take any decisions or actions based on this false identity.

Me: Although I experienced my true, limitless nature, most of my actions yesterday were carried out with the same old belief. Like, I was so tired with all my college activities that I just dozed off as soon as I reached home. I could have completed some of my pending tasks, but I didn't.

As you said, we have all been deeply programmed with the belief that I am the body. Is there a way to undo this programming and detach ourself from the body?

Success: Yes, there is an easy way to do so. Consider your body to be your friend and treat it in that manner. For your friend, you say, "He is my friend;" likewise you can say about your body, "This body is my friend." If you feel hungry, say in your mind, "My friend is hungry, not me." If you feel tired, say, "My friend is tired, not me; as I am full of energy." After knowing your true nature, when you see something happening to your body, you won't say that it is happening with you. Instead, you will say, "This is happening to the friend I have with me." Try practicing this in every small activity.

Me: That means when I treat it as my friend, I will not identify with it.

Success: Correct. This understanding about your body will weaken your attachment with the body.

When you were a child, you were very clear that you are not the body. Just as children are clearly able to see that they are not the body, similarly if you too start seeing yourself in that manner, then you will use the body to fulfill your actual purpose. Whenever you use the word "I," you will be aware. Then your actions will not be carried out in unconsciousness. All your thoughts and actions will arise from the understanding of who you truly are. And so will your decisions. The point is, as long as you don't know that you have got this body, this body hasn't got you, you will live with this mistaken identity.

CONVERSATION 14

Me: I really have to practice a lot!

Success: You may find it that way in the beginning. However, the secret is **CONSISTENCY**. Don't fall into the trap of judging or criticizing yourself for failing or succeeding in this practice. Keep practicing it every day, consistently. Then, automatically, a day will come when you will find that you have already started living your life with the right understanding of your true nature.

Me: So, whatever may happen, I need to constantly remind myself that this body is my friend and whatever is happening is actually happening with my friend?

Success: Exactly. But give lots of love to your body. Talk positively about your body. Accept it with all its positives and negatives. Think about how you can use the positive qualities of your body for creating something higher on this planet. Love your body for its shortcomings and take steps for overcoming them. When you love your friend, you always wish for his or her well-being. Similarly, strive for the well-being of your body. Nourish it with healthy food and give it the right amount of rest and exercise.

Train your body for the higher purpose instead of indulging in unhealthy entertainment like TV, social media, porn, parties, smoking, drinking, etc. There are much more wonderful things on this planet that will give you true joy rather than ruining your life in the endless pursuit of unhealthy entertainment. Increase the efficiency and efficacy of your friend. Enhance its skills and capabilities to help you in your Self Expression.

Do whatever needs to be done for your friend. But do not consider it as your personal problem. Whatever is happening with the body, whichever incident has taken place, it may even be pain in the body, remember: "It is all happening with my friend, not me." And as I said earlier, do whatever it takes to keep your body healthy. This is because you are not the body but you are with the body.

Me: So, this is about being detached from the body. But as you said, God or Self has a purpose behind creating this body. The Self wants to experience and express itself through this body. What should I do to fulfil this ultimate purpose?

Success: This auspicious thought is the divine sign of transformation. To fulfil the ultimate purpose, carry out your spiritual practice or *sadhana* earnestly. Bring 'Who am I? Meditation' into regular practice. This will take you in the state of inner silence or *moun*, which is the state of stillness intrinsic to the Self. It is the state beyond sound and silence, beyond thought and speech.

Use your inertia to make your body sit at one place for meditation. Interestingly, meditation uses inertia to kill inertia. When a person sits to meditate, he sits inertly, in one position, without moving. In this situation, the body does not have any work other than to sit. As you reach the depths of meditation, you will realize, "This is a body, and I am separate from it. I am limitless." This conviction will help you in every aspect of life— including getting rid of the tendency of lethargy.

Me: It means I have to use lethargy to overcome lethargy. That is the best use of lethargy!

Success: Yes. At the next step, feel the love for the Self. Reading and listening to the supreme truth will arouse love for the Self. Love for the Self is divine devotion, which has great power. It is due to love that a mother gets up in the middle of the night for her child. She is on her toes even if she does not get enough sleep. When it comes to her child, she does not worry about sleep or rest because she loves her child.

Me: This means once I start experiencing the love for the Self, I will give a chance to the Self to express through my body, instead of serving lethargy. I will 3 operate from the source of energy inside me. I will always be bubbling with life!

Success: Fabulous! Let me tell you about a devotee, who immersed in God's love, wished to build a beautiful temple for God. However, he could not do so because of his financial condition. So, he thought, "If I cannot build a temple, I will at least try to make my body a temple." And he did so, with the power of devotion. In the same way, imagine what good you could embrace if the same desire were aroused in you! You would constantly ponder over which tendencies need to be thrown out to purify your temple and which qualities need to be developed to adorn your temple. If those thoughts are always in your mind, everything will happen easily through your body and you won't feel lethargic. All of this is possible with the power of devotion.

When you earnestly carry out spiritual practice, you experience this power. There may be varying circumstances, but you will always respond according to your spiritual master's commands. If devotion has awakened within you, it is easy to follow your master's commands and acquire mastery over passivity. This is because only after devotion awakens within you, you actually understand what needs to be done and you start doing it. You must have seen or read about the extent to which one goes to show one's love for one's beloved. Now, think of how much more one can do when inspired by divine love! A life filled with true devotion eliminates all bad habits, including sloth. Hence, work earnestly towards the highest level of spirituality, which is inner stillness and devotion. This will make your body the best temple.

Me: Aha! I never thought of my body as a temple; but it really is, and I want to treat it that way.

Success: Amen. :)

❂❂❂

MY SACRED TEMPLE

If you want to make your body a temple, the first condition is to eliminate excess lethargy.

The cause of lethargy in some people is unbalanced dietary habits. Excessive and wrong eating habits cause weight gain to the point where such people find it difficult to even move their body a little. Such people need to consult a dietician to improve their diet.

Observe which foods you are consuming that increase inertia and which foods aid in reducing inertia. If a lethargic person becomes aware and understands this, he will find it very easy to control his lethargy. Let us look at some examples.

1. If I know that junk food as well as soft and hard drinks add lethargy to my body, then how frequently will I fall prey to these temptations?

   o Once in a fortnight

   o Once in a month

   o Once in a quarter

o Never

2. To maintain the purity of my temple (body), I will follow a diet that consists of:

o Green leafy vegetables

o Fruits

o Salads

o Home-made meals

Now that you have planned your diet, stick to it no matter what, and it will pay huge dividends. Also remember that above all it is devotion that can give you the strength to become active again and make your body a temple. The very thought "My body is a temple" will automatically keep you away from the temptations of overeating and junk food. If devotion is missing and your diet is also heavy, then the body will definitely slip into inactivity and disease.

QUOTES

Prayer is the greatest power
which has been given
to man even before
problems arise in his life.

~ Sirshree ~

Prayer is the invisible
solution to every problem
in life.

~ Sirshree ~

After a heartfelt prayer,
you won't have to
solve problems.
You will see them getting
solved automatically.

~ Sirshree ~

CONVERSATION 15

Me: Good morning, Success! I have heard, "Ask and you shall receive." My question is, how do I ask and whom do I ask?

Success: Ask nature, pray to nature. Nature always helps you to heal your body and mind. And since prayer is a miraculous tool, we are going to learn how to pray for attaining freedom from excess passivity. It is the easiest and most effective way to get rid of lethargy. You can call it the 'E Body Prayer'.

Me: 'E Body'... like email?

Success: 😁 Not exactly, but that was a great guess. Let me explain. The human body is composed of five basic elements: air, ether, fire, water and earth. Among these five elements, the earth element is responsible for passivity in the body. Hence, we are going to pray to the earth element present in your body—referred to here as E body (E = earth)—to remove excess passivity from your body. If you pray with complete faith and understanding, you shall definitely get 100% result. Therefore, offer this prayer consistently.

Here's the right way to offer this prayer. Sit down and close your eyes. Then address the earth element of your body and communicate with it using the following steps.

1. Invite: "My dear, divine E body, I invite you into my field of attention."

2. Declare: "Dear E body, you can heal yourself and I can heal myself. You, I, and all the masters of the universe together can heal the entire universe. We all have so much power. You have the power to remove excess passivity from the body."

3. Pray: "Dear E body, there should be perfect balance between passivity, hyperactivity and equanimity. You can help make this body suitable for the highest expression of the Self by shedding the excess passivity. You have the power and the strength. I have complete faith in your powers. Hence, please begin to release the excess passivity."

4. Inform: "Dear E body, even after you leave my field of attention, please continue with this, until you have shed all the excess passivity."

5. Permit: "Dear E body, love, bliss and stillness have immense power; hence allow them to help you in getting rid of excess passivity."

6. Chant: Imagine love, bliss and stillness in the form of rays of light entering your body and helping your body to release the lethargy. Keep chanting for at least two minutes: "Love... Bliss... Stillness... Love... Bliss... Stillness..." Feel the wonderful experience of love, bliss and stillness.

7. Thank: Finally, say, "I am grateful to you, E body, for all your support. Now you can go back to your place. Thank you...thank you... thank you..."

This was the E body prayer, which is highly effective. You

can memorize it and practice it at any time of the day.

Me: Wow! That was something unique! I shall definitely practice it daily and see the results. Are there any more special prayers you can tell me about?

Success: I can tell you one more special type of prayer, which is done in the following manner.

Stand up and close your eyes. Now very slowly whirl yourself round and round. You can open your arms towards the sky or you can join your hands while whirling or adopt any position of the hands that makes you feel more receptive.

Me: Just like Sufi whirling, right?

Success: Kind of, but your whirling has got to be very, very slow as compared to Sufi whirling. And as said, adopt that position of your hands which makes you feel receptive. Now imagine a divine white light showering on your body and receive this divine light within you. In this prayer, the understanding is that the earth element in your body is getting activated and its frequency is increasing, due to which the excess lethargy is being eliminated. Excess lethargy is related to the earth element, hence your intention should be: "This divine white light is washing away all excess passivity from my body-mind and making it eligible for the experience and expression of the Self."

If you have understood the importance of this and if you are ready, then you will offer this prayer from the depth of your heart.

Whirl at a very slow speed or at a speed that feels right to you. With every rotation, imagine that your body is receiving the healing light and releasing laziness and other negativities. Pray that this divine white light is benefitting you as well as everyone else in this world. With this prayer meditation, you will find that your frequency and eligibility for attaining your ultimate goal is increasing. Your inner strength is increasing. The excess passivity in your body-mind is being released and only the required amount remains in the body. Continue to whirl slowly.

With the feeling of joy and love, express gratitude to the Almighty, saying, "Thank you dear God, thank you… thank you…!"

With this prayer, you can easily get rid of excess lethargy and transform your body into a temple—pure and sacred.

After this prayer, you can open your eyes and continue with your usual activities with the feeling of happiness and love inside.

Me: Wow! This feels awesome!! You have put it in such simple words. It's a prayer in the true sense because there is clear understanding as to what I am asking for and why I am asking it. When and how often can I offer this prayer?

Success: This is not a ritual. You can do it any time, but make sure you are in a peaceful state when you do it. If you practice it every day, you will get great benefits. It will remind you about your higher aim of attaining the attributeless state. It will keep you active all day. Consistency in these prayers will help to manifest the result faster and you will start feeling light. The more you experience lightness inside, the more you may want to free yourself from even the remaining excess lethargy. Once you find that much of the excess lethargy has been shed, you can practice this prayer meditation as and when needed.

Once you understand the complete prayer, you can also sing the following prayer while whirling.

My body is whirling round and round.

Divine white light is showering on it.

I am receiving and absorbing that divine light.

All the negativity in this body is fading away.

The earth element in my body, you have the power.

You can release the excess passivity.

You can end this lethargy.

So, please begin.

And even after going out of my field of attention,

please continue this until all excess passivity is released.

Now you may go back to your place.

Thank you... Thank you... Thank you...

Me: Thank you!

HEAL YOURSELF

Seek help from the Self within. Pray to it for inner strength to work religiously on getting rid of laziness. Also seek forgiveness for having harbored this harmful tendency in your body till date. Forgiveness is the ultimate tool of healing. It has the power to completely heal your body and mind. You can take help of the following words to heal yourself and to release lethargy.

I now truly want to get established in
the attributeless state.
I want to be supremely successful by achieving
the ultimate purpose of my life.
Please bless me with inner strength so that I can consistently work towards liberating myself from   excess
passivity until I attain the attributeless state.
Please forgive me for my ignorance and for
harboring this tendency in my body.
I am now happily releasing all those core thoughts that
were strengthening this laziness pattern.
Please free me from this bondage of lethargy and
make me worthy of your grace so that I can fulfill
my purpose of coming to Earth.
Thank you... Thank you... Thank you.

You are destined to Succeed!

Having received such beautiful prayers and techniques, Ankit felt as if his level of consciousness had climbed the Everest. He felt extremely happy and confident that he could now achieve whatever he wanted.

The next day when he was chatting with Success, he said, "With such higher wisdom and prayers, I feel like I've received some superpowers."

"Or perhaps the superpowers inherent within you are awakening," replied Success.

"I guess so. I still remember what you said when we spoke for the first time: Everything is naturally flowing towards me. Those words are still ringing in my ears. Does this mean everyone is destined for success?"

"Absolutely. Progress is a natural phenomenon. Nature automatically pushes man towards success. When you deeply meditate on this, you will find that everybody is progressing automatically. It is only the demons of the mind—anger, envy, hatred, greed, sloth, negative thinking, ego, and the like—that block an individual's way. Once you free yourself from all these demons, you would achieve the ultimate success. Thereby, you will find yourself successful in all areas of life—career, relations, health, financials and spiritual. You open up all the divine possibilities of your body-mind for the highest expression of the Self. The moment you come to know your true self, recognize the powers hidden within you, give your thoughts the right direction, and make the most of nature's bounty, you would enter the realm of success. You will be tuned to the natural flow of love, joy, health, wealth, peace, creativity and all the divine qualities of the Self. Remember, success is your nature. You are bound to be supremely successful!"

"Woohoo! And that's why you had said that you are even more eager to show up in my life."

"Yes. And I feel that now you are ready for me. You have already achieved the first success."

"I have?! What?"

"You have successfully completed the 15 days of our interaction that we had agreed upon. I'm so proud of you that you went against your strongest tendency and continued to converse with me. I must say that you have been an excellent student! I give you an A+."

"Oh, thank you! I am proud of me too. It wasn't easy to wake up early every day, but I love your company... But are you saying this is our last day? Does this mean you're no longer going to chat with me?!"

"Hey, don't worry. We may not chat in this manner, but we could always be together if you want to."

"I definitely want to! I'm never going to let you go. And you have taught me how to do that."

"I am pleased, my mission is complete. But can I ask you do something?"

"Certainly."

"Can you prepare a chart of all the main points we have discussed, so that you won't forget them?"

"That's an excellent idea! I have been making notes after every conversation we've had and I've also started to implement the action plans you have given me. So, it would be fairly easy to prepare a summary. I shall definitely do it."

"That's great! Work towards success and you shall definitely achieve it. And don't stop at that. Strive with all your heart to achieve your ultimate purpose, because that's ultimate success. Then help others also to attain it and spread happiness among people. And that's my ultimate purpose."

"What a wonderful purpose you have! If everybody does this, it'll make our world simply AMAZING! I'll surely fulfill my ultimate purpose as well as yours."

"I'm so happy to hear that! My work here is done. And now, dear Ankit, it's time for me to stop speaking and you to start working, so that we can always be close friends."

"Ohhh! You are the bestest friend anybody could ever wish for. You have shown me my true nature and how to go about life. I've got so used to you... I'm going to miss you terribly. But let me thank you with all my heart. You have literally saved my life! Thank you soooo much, dear Success. This has been an incredible journey. But NO, I am not letting you go. Fasten your seatbelt. I'm ready to throw out laziness and go for the ride of my life! And I'm expecting you to be with me every step of the way!"

"I'm right there with you, my friend!"

***

As promised, Ankit made a chart of the summary.

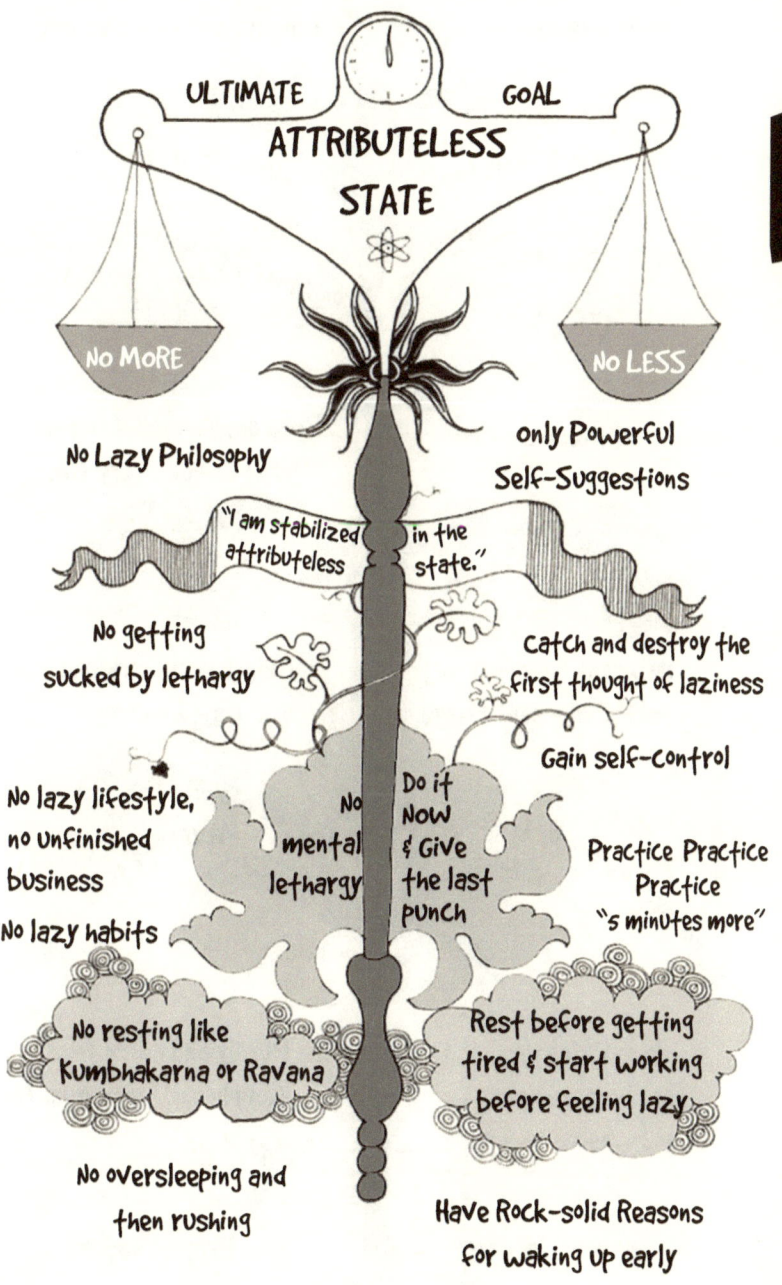

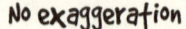

The next day, Ankit woke up at the usual time that he had been for the past 15 days. "Hello! Good morning!" He said, looking expectantly at the trophy. But no, Success did not speak back. Well, no harm in trying, he thought. He felt a bit lost and didn't know what to do. Then, still looking at the trophy, he knew what he was supposed to do.

He got ready and was coming out of his room when he heard his parents and his brother talking at the breakfast table. He inadvertently stopped to listen.

"I have heard him talking in his room early in the mornings. I've knocked a few times but he's always ignored. I think he's officially lost it!" said Rohit. Ankit chuckled softly.

"Rohit! That's not the way to speak about your elder brother!... Well, I don't know what he's up to but he seems happier. And I'm glad that he's been waking up early and going to college on time," said his mother. Ankit smiled.

"I too have observed some positive changes in his behaviour and attitude..." his father was saying, which pleased Ankit.

He opened the front door and was leaving, when his mother heard and called out, "Ankit! Where are you going? Come and have some breakfast."

"I'm not hungry right now, mom. I have something important to do... I'll eat something later on."

"But..."

"Bye, mom." Ankit left quickly, still smiling.

***

"Nice trophy, Ankit! How... I mean when did you get it?"

"Actually, it's yours! I had taken it during your party and I'm very very sorry for that..." Ankit apologized profusely and explained everything to Vihaan, who was baffled and a bit angry, but eventually gave in. "It's okay, man! I understand," he said. But he looked distracted and tensed.

CONVERSATION 15

"What's the matter, Vihaan?" asked Ankit.

"What can I tell you? There's so much going on. We still have the final exams, and then there's the pressure of Harvard. I have been checking out their syllabus and the schedules... it's crazy! And the kind of students over there... how can I compete with them? Everybody expects me to always top everything! How can I do it? And the amount of money my father has to spend... it's driving me nuts! What if I can't deliver?"

"Hey, calm down, bro..."

"That's easy to say... you know I simply cannot study due to all this pressure... If I continue this way, I won't even pass the finals..."

Ankit was seeing in reality what Success had discussed with him. At this point, he felt the actual significance of the teachings he had received, and how important it was for everyone to know them.

"Hey, Vihaan! Don't worry, man! You have always succeeded and you always will. Do you know why you've succeeded till date? Because you have enjoyed the process! Success and happiness—both are important. But now you're allowing so many thoughts to paralyze you. You are allowing other people and factors to influence you. But do you know that nobody and nothing can influence you unless you allow them to? So, just shoo off all these draining thoughts. Then focus only on what you want and everything will be just fine. Do what you always do. Work your magic and the results will be magical again."

"You're right, man! I think I've been over-thinking it... And since when did you get so smart?!" asked Vihaan with a smile. They had been close friends in their childhood but later as Ankit had fallen back in studies, they had somehow grown apart. Ankit had started preferring the company of his own kind. But now they both felt close again.

"Hahaha... Did you think that you're the only smart guy in the world? Jokes apart, I can tell you that a very good friend has been helping me out. You don't know him... or actually you do... but you need to know more about him or it..."

"What are you blabbering, man? Whom are you talking about?"

"Well, I'll tell you about it sometime. Now let's go, we don't want to be late for college." Ankit smiled and thought, "I can't help anybody much at this time. But I hope very soon I'll achieve success and then help fulfill what Success wants. Success wants me to help others achieve success and happiness. Soon...very soon... it's going to happen..."

✺ ✺ ✺

APPENDIX

FAQS ON LETHARGY
(ANSWERS BY SIRSHREE)

Q1: I usually carry out all my daily work in a good frame of mind. Planning for the next day also takes place smoothly. I know that actually I'm not doing anything; God is working through me. Hence I feel relaxed. However, if someone gives me a set of long-term goals—say, a list of projects to be completed over the next six months—my first thought is: "How can I do all this in six months?! How is it possible?" It creates too much pressure and, therefore, it takes too much time to even begin the work. So, how do I get rid of this stress?

A: A clock is programmed to tick every second. That's 3,600 seconds an hour, 86,400 ticks a day and 31,536,000 ticks a year. And a clock ticks on and on, for years on end. Can you imagine what would happen if clocks were living creatures, and if someone told a new clock the number of times it would have to tick in its lifetime? A heart attack! That's what the number would do to it. It would be totally tensed thinking, "How will I ever tick that many times?!"

If you get a similar question about the number of activities you have to perform, you should remind yourself: "It's true that I have to work my whole life, but at one time I have to do only one task." Focus on the task at hand and do not worry about the next task to be done. Let your plans follow their own course. While working on the plan, if you suddenly feel the need for improvisation, it will happen on its own. This is the beauty of nature, and once you understand it, you will begin to see things falling into place.

Some people avoid wearing a watch, as merely looking at it stresses them out. So, if you don't want that to happen with you, just understand that you have to do only one thing at a time. Everyone has to work in some way or the other throughout their life. Finishing one project does not mean all your work is finished. The reality is, even you want to be always active. You want to engage your body in some activity, so that it can be of service, wherever and however you are.

Actually, you are putting your body to use by being who you really are: the Universal Self. As the Self, your understanding is: *I have to always derive happiness from everything and I have to spread happiness. I have to spread happiness by being happiness itself.* This means, working should make you happy and you should carry out every activity happily. Therefore, don't think you will get happiness only when you finish your work. If you remember that the aim is to be happy, you'll never face any difficulties while performing any job. Every secret will unfold at its time, but you have to do just one thing at a time. Mistakes are likely to happen when you take up two thoughts or two jobs simultaneously.

If you are singing a song and someone tells you to sing the same song to the tune of a new song, you may begin with it but the earlier tune is likely to keep intruding. In this case, you would tell yourself to focus on the new tune, and not on the old tune. Likewise, focus on the new in other aspects of your life as well. All the time, give your attention to whatever new is appearing before you. If you do this, you will not even realize how the six months flew by and all the work was beautifully accomplished on its own. You will feel happy. This will help you develop the faith that you have to live life one task at a time. Plan for six months but carry out just the task at hand. Do not be anxious thinking about the future. Remember this and you will not have any difficulties in completing your work.

Q2: I know that the mission of Tej Gyan Foundation [which is based on Sirshree's teachings] is to raise the consciousness level of Earth and transform this world into a highly evolved society. I am lazy and I tend to postpone every task. My question is, what kind of a person lives in a highly evolved society? How should his actions be and how would he shift to the supreme level of consciousness with *maya* (cosmic illusion or worldly attractions) surrounding him?

A: In a highly evolved society, people are honest and sincere. In such a society, you have total faith that no one will take advantage of your weakness. Therefore, if you clearly state your problem without any deceit and ask for help, you will receive genuine guidance.

When you fall sick, you visit a doctor. The doctor asks you questions, checks you and reaches a diagnosis. He then informs you about your ailment and gives you various treatment options. Similarly, there are various ways to break down excess passivity. In an evolved society, you can talk to counsellors and well-wishers who will help you to take the necessary steps to overcome your wrong tendencies.

However, this does not mean that evolved people don't have wrong tendencies. They do, but they know that they have to always choose the highest option. They also know that merely looking after the conveniences and comforts of the body will not support the Self to express through their bodies or prepare them to participate in the supreme creation by the Self. They have a natural inclination to make the highest choices and to resolve problems.

When you find that your vehicle is not performing optimally, you take it to the garage to get it fixed. Accordingly, if the body has developed lethargy, there are people to guide you. You don't have to be afraid that they will take advantage of you if they know your weakness. This is because people in a highly evolved society perform their duties as a higher form of *seva* (*seva* means serving others as if there is no other). They have chosen to offer these services. They undergo training and preparation in every way before offering these services. As a result, in a highly evolved society, if somebody's level of consciousness goes down, he participates in particular retreats, which are arranged as refresher courses on the available wisdom and techniques. These retreats help to raise his level of consciousness and provide the cure for his problems. Those who are clear about their ultimate aim in life take maximum benefit of these retreats. The collective impact of these retreats uplifts society.

Q3: I always feel, "Let me do things at a leisurely and comfortable pace, nobody should pressure me into hurrying up." But now this tendency is creating obstacles, due to which I cannot complete any task. I'm also not able to make any firm decisions that this is what I want and this is what I should do. My confidence dips further when I look at other people's lives. As a result, lethargy takes a hold of me again and I evade work. But I also keep on thinking, "Even I want what my colleague has... my friend is going for a foreign trip, I too should do the same..." Please guide me on how to tackle this problem.

A: Your question has raised two points. The first is laziness and the second is that your decisions and thoughts keep changing looking at what people around you are doing. You have to work on both aspects. In order to liberate yourself from lethargy, you should use your willpower to do your work. Every day, perform those actions which the mind tries to duck out of. Thereby, as soon as some work presents before you and you get the thought, "I can do it tomorrow; not today," perform one or two actions related to that work then and there. This practice will help reduce indolence until it eventually disappears.

Everyone has different lifestyles these days. Some children face difficulties due to the way they are raised. Some people don't even realize that their parenting style of too much pampering is aiding the development of excess passivity in their children. So, later on they have to spend so much time to get rid of that passivity.

It's essential to remove that excess passivity and hence one needs to start working on eradicating it at some point. As hard as it may seem, ask what you can do today, and do that. You have to incorporate a workout or yoga into your schedule along with your daily chores. This keeps the body healthy and energetic and also helps to reduce lethargy. Therefore, ask yourself, "Am I doing all of these or not?" If your answer is, "No," then you have to start immediately.

You have been asked to practice yoga because many passive people also have a thirst for the Truth. Such people should do yoga and pranayam regularly in order to free themselves from inertia and attain the Truth. Doing it little by little, every day, will develop this habit. The Guru encourages you to cultivate such good habits because he sees your potential.

Keep it in mind that lethargy may embarrass you when you have attained some status in your life and people consider you as their idol. At present you may think, "Everyone does this; this is how life is, and this is how it will always be," and you may continue behaving like everyone else. Other people will not be able to guide you as they too think along the same lines. The Guru wants you to attain your highest potential and also protect you from those habits that would embarrass you when you realize that people consider you their role model. The Guru wants you to reach the highest level, from where you can gloriously claim: "My life is an open book and I have led it in a beautiful manner." The book of your life should inspire people, who will then decide to lead a similar life. They will think that if you have attained so much, if you could pull yourself together in spite of all the difficult circumstances, then so can they. And their confidence will increase. Always keep in mind that the Guru sees your actual potential and accordingly he does not want you to make mistakes that you would repent in the future.

People don't know who they will turn out to be. Imagine there is a person who does not know who he will become—whether the Buddha, or Mahavira or Mahatma Gandhi. He lives his life imitating others. And then when he reaches a particular stature in life, his past begins to bother him. He thinks, "If only I had known that I had such a noble role to play in life, I wouldn't have made such mistakes in the past. I would not have cultivated bad habits like drinking, smoking or drugs."

In order to be prepared for any future greatness, you have to tell yourself that from now on, what, when, where, how and how much you are going to do. Along with yourself, you should also be able to tell others, "We can be our true self and experience our beingness, wherever we are." Once you realize this, you can inspire others too. However, you will need to consistently work on yourself in order to do so.

Even though laziness is an impediment for you today, you can still carry out some of your work. Most people end up choosing one of the two extremes. They spend most of their time thinking and end up doing nothing, or they simply choose to do nothing at all. You don't have to get into either extremes. The only way to avoid them is to put in a little work every day. This will develop the habit of hard work, since all habits develop when they are worked upon consistently.

You may have noticed that new books are seen almost every month in book stores and book exhibitions. Have you ever wondered how and why this happens? This is because some people are consistently working on creating those books. They work upon the discourses or speeches delivered by great people and present the wisdom derived from those in a suitable manner. These books reach you because of those people's devotion, dedication and diligent efforts. They put in at least a little work every day, so that you can use the guidance from these books to gain the highest benefits. The Guru wants you to develop similar work habits. If you can make a habit of reading those books, even one paragraph at a time, you will sow the seeds of enthusiasm and zeal within you to cast off inertia as well as be saved from getting into wrong things looking at the world around you. You will then be able to carry out your highest work and become an inspiration for others to attain their highest potential.

Q4: Sirshree, I attended the Magic of Awakening Retreat conducted by Tej Gyan Foundation. I continue to read your teachings and listen to your discourses. However, I sometimes find it difficult to implement those teachings due to laziness. While the initial thought is to do every activity at the proper time, lethargy soon sets in, and I start thinking, "I can do this tomorrow." When I meet or hear of someone sincerely carrying out their spiritual practice *(sadhana)*, I think, "If he's doing it, I will also try to do it," but that doesn't happen. How do I take my learning from the retreat into my practical life?

A: As you already know, listening to discourses and contemplating on them is one of the important steps for realizing the Truth. The other is to intensify your thirst for attaining the Truth and getting liberation from the cosmic illusion *(maya)*. You have to deepen your love and devotion for liberation. Unless this love exists, one remains sluggish even after gaining knowledge of the Truth.

If someone listens to discourses but does not have the thirst for liberation, he thinks, "All this makes good sense, but it's my family members who should be listening to it." But if he listens to the Truth consistently, he grows spiritually. He then realizes that he is the one who is supposed to act on the wisdom and guidance being imparted in the discourses. Consequently, he wants to work on the guidance, but his lethargy becomes an obstacle and impedes his progress. So, he thinks, "This is very useful knowledge, I will definitely work on it later on." This happens because his desire for the Truth is not intense enough as yet. The love required for liberation is not strong enough. He has a different assumption about liberation, and hence does not feel the need for it. He does not even think about what his purpose on Earth is and why or how much time he has to fulfill it. If you think about it, the time you spend here on Earth is minuscule compared to the length of the afterlife in the astral world. You may have 80 or 100 years here on Earth. You might think this is long enough to understand and attain the Truth. However, if you look at it from the higher angle, this lifetime will seem very small.

Now it is important to understand the reference point of your thinking. If you are having trouble implementing the teachings despite having gained wisdom in the retreat and discourses, then examine your point of reference. Suppose you have a glass of water in front of you, but you aren't very thirsty. What happens? You don't pick it up to drink it, right? Similarly, if your thirst for the Truth has not developed intensely or if you are more interested in what is going on in the material world, then you are unable to take steps towards the Truth.

Therefore, start working immediately on the activities that you are expected to. If this does not happen, it simply means you haven't understood some part of the teachings clearly. There are many people who claim, "I have understood everything," but no transformation is seen in their life. So, even if you have understood something, it's likely that your understanding is not deep enough and lacks seriousness. You have not absorbed the profundity of the Truth yet. When you attain conviction about the Truth, there will be no reason left for sorrow in your life. You will be free from every sorrow or misery. You will ask yourself, "Is this particular sorrow worth spending even one moment extra over it?" and your answer will be, "No."

However, one's mind demands proof when one is not convinced about the Truth. So, you have to keep giving it more and more proof that liberation and transcendence is your ultimate aim. You came to Earth to attain this very aim. Life has already been giving you various indications about this.

You just haven't decoded them. Now if you recollect once again the blessings and the grace that is being showered upon you, your thirst for the Truth will intensify. Many people don't even know that there is a spiritual foundation that prepares you to attain the highest purpose of human life—the seventh or supreme level of consciousness. When they come to know this, they will also seek admission in Tej Gyan Foundation so as to reach the highest level of consciousness.

For that to happen, your desire to attain the Truth should strengthen. Once that happens, you will find that new experiments are being done by you every day. Until your mind comprehends the teachings completely, learn to take small steps to become disciplined. You may encounter lethargy along the way, but you have to first head towards hyperactivity, then to equanimity and finally onto the attributeless state. This is the actual path for growth. You get opportunities to end your inertia every day. If you work on it, you can pat yourself on the back, saying, "This is good! I have managed to perform at least some part of the work despite the laziness." In this way, your confidence will go on rising day by day.

If you have understood all these aspects and are still unable to implement them, tell your mind, "You haven't understood yet. Had you understood, it would have percolated in your actions." From afar, a piece of rope can appear to be a terrifying snake. However, if you go ahead and take a closer look, you will realize it's just a piece of rope and you will start laughing. However, if you are afraid of going ahead, you will never realize you had mistaken a rope for a snake.

Conclusion: The mind initially makes excuses to avoid spiritual practice thinking it to be difficult or tedious, but when you understand the need for the Truth and its high priority, you can question your mind's excuses instead of going along with them. Once you begin your spiritual practice, you will find it simple and easy to practice.

Q5: How does the Guru's grace work in lethargic people?

A: When the whip of the Guru's grace cracks (symbolically), the indolent body-mind comes under control. Just like a mahout controls his elephant by jabbing at its head, the Guru too plays different roles for different people.

The Guru is equivalent to a whip for those who are overly passive. And a whip (symbolically) is required to keep lethargic people active. A lethargic person will not run if he can walk, he will not walk if he can get away with standing, he will not stand if he can sit, and he will not even sit if he can lie down. He needs grace or else he will remain the same.

Initially, he will not realize the grace in the Guru's whip. Indolence within an individual demands unconsciousness and inertia. It wants something that will induce some degree of unconsciousness, which will make it feel good. It longs for new experiences which can do that, leading the individual to smoking, drinking and drugs. With these demands, its inner craving is for dullness. A lethargic person enjoys dullness and constantly searches for it. In this scenario, the Guru orders him to practice breathing exercises or *pranayam* in order to maintain the body's balance. Initially, the mind does not comply, but the love you have for the Guru and for yourself, leads you to exercise.

Pranayam involves taking deep, long breaths, which is highly beneficial for the entire body and the mind. It is an offering you will give yourself if you love yourself. Otherwise, inertia can even make breathing seem like a task. As a result, a person takes short breaths, instead of taking long ones. Therefore, make a conscious effort to love yourself, and practice it by taking deep breaths. With this, passivity takes a beating and you can replace your laziness with new possibilities. Beyond passivity lie hyperactivity and equanimity, and at the centre lies the attributeless state. You have to balance all three attributes to reach this state of transcendence.

Q6: Sirshree, I am going through a phase in which I just don't feel like doing anything. I am not taking the required steps for progress. My life is moving at a snail's pace. You always say, "Every scene is a preparation for the next." So, if this is today's scene, what will tomorrow's be like? Why am I in this state of mind? How can I change it?

A: If Sirshree tells you what to do, will you do it, or will you say, "I just can't. I can't help it"? We will move ahead only if your answer is "yes." So, what do you say?

Seeker: Yes! I will follow your guidance.

Sirshree: Fine. Then, to begin with, take baby steps. Know that the work which the mind is not willing to do is actually your food for thought. You have to think over it and consider this period as the first interval of your life. This is because you are in the midst of an interval and are not doing the work that you should be doing during this phase. In this case, ask your mind, "How long you'll take to complete this particular work? If you were to practice meditation, how long can you sit? 5 minutes? 10? 20? For how long can you read the literature on Truth? How many times can you pray? How much time can you dedicate to work related to home, studies, and other things?" Decide a minimum amount of time for all these activities. That way, when you successfully carry out a given activity, your confidence will receive a boost.

Those who want to strengthen their confidence will decide to finish the work at hand, say, on the very same day. And then they will do it. As a result, their confidence will shoot up. If you too start with and successfully complete small tasks first, you will find that you can accomplish any task—no matter how big it seems.

A baby is passive in the womb. Yet, the baby grows progressively because it is in the attributeless state—in the state of beingness. Due to passivity, if you are not doing anything and also if you are not in the state of beingness, then it does not work for you. You do not progress.

Now you need to learn a little about hyperactivity. If a body is hyperactive, it can come and go anywhere and perform any work. Little by little, learn to move from passivity toward semi-passivity—the state between passivity and hyperactivity. It will subsequently be easier to reach the state of hyperactivity. From there, the journey is towards semi- hyperactivity, then equanimity, followed by semi-equanimity and then finally the attributeless state. All this would be easier if you go step by step. In the attributeless state, you make effective use of all the three basic attributes. Passivity can help you sit peacefully in meditation, hyperactivity can be used for carrying out work, and equanimity can help you to contribute towards social welfare.

The main lesson here is that you will use all three attributes, but your ultimate aim is to be detached from them, i.e. to attain the attributeless state.

You are at level one at present. Now decide the small steps which will take you from level one to level two. Ask your mind, "How long can you work on this particular task?" If it says, "I can work on it for 5 minutes at the most," then make sure it works for 5 minutes, every day, consistently. This will progressively raise your confidence, and the quality and quantity of your activities will also increase as compared to before.

All the above-mentioned points are applicable to everyone and are especially relevant for the youth. Many young people are aimless because they cannot decide what they want to do. Therefore, you yourself need to decide your aim. Ask yourself, "What do I want to do? What is the meaning of my life?" You have to find out which work makes you happy. Ask yourself, "What is my aim? I have to determine my aim till this particular date." Once you have set your aim, you will see all aspects of your life attaining completion within the time-frame you had set for them.

✲ ✲ ✲

About Sirshree

Sirshree's spiritual quest, which began during his childhood, led him on a journey through various schools of philosophy and meditation practices. He studied a wide range of literature on mind science and spirituality. After a long period of deep contemplation on the truth of life, his quest culminated in attaining the ultimate truth.

Sirshree espouses, "All spiritual paths that lead to the truth begin differently but culminate at the same point – Understanding. This understanding is complete in itself. Listening to this understanding is enough to attain the Truth." Over the last two decades, he has dedicated his life to raising mass consciousness.

Sirshree has delivered more than 4000 discourses that throw light on this understanding. He has designed a system for wisdom, which makes it accessible to all. This system has inspired people from all walks of life to progress on their journey of the Truth. Thousands of seekers join in a virtual prayer for World Peace and Global Healing daily at 9:09 am and 9:09 pm.

About Tej Gyan Foundation

Tej Gyan Foundation is a non-profit organization founded on the teachings of Sirshree. The Foundation disseminates Tejgyan – the wisdom that guides one from self-development to Self-realization, leading towards Self-stabilization.

The Foundation's system for imparting wisdom has been assessed by international quality auditors and accredited with the ISO 9001:2015 certification. This wisdom has been presented in a simple, systematic, and practically applicable form that makes it accessible to people from all walks of life, regardless of religion, caste, social strata, country, or belief system.

The Foundation has centers in more than 400 cities and towns across India and other countries. The mission of Tej Gyan Foundation is to create a highly evolved society by leading seekers from negative to positive thoughts and further, from positive thoughts to Happy thoughts. A 'Happy thought' is the auspicious thought of being free from all thoughts, leading to the state of supreme bliss beyond thoughts.

If you seek such wisdom that leads you beyond mere knowledge, dissolves all problems, frees you from all limiting beliefs, reveals the true nature of divinity, and establishes you in the ultimate truth, then it is time to discover Tejgyan; it is time to rise above the mundane knowledge of words and experience Tejgyan!

The MahaAasmani Magic of Awakening Retreat

Self-development to Self-realization towards Self-stabilization

Do you wish to experience unconditional happiness that is not dependent on any reason? Happiness that is permanent and only increases with time? Do you wish to experience love, peace, self-belief, harmony in relationships, prosperity, and true contentment? Do you wish to progress in all facets of your life, viz. physical, mental, social, financial, and spiritual?

If you seek answers to these questions and are thirsty for the ultimate truth, then you are welcome to participate in the MahaAasmani Magic of Awakening retreat organized by Tej Gyan Foundation. This is the Foundation's flagship retreat based on the teachings of Sirshree.

The Purpose of this Retreat

The purpose of this retreat is that every human being should:

- Discover the answer to "Who am I" and "Why am I?" through direct experience and be established in ultimate bliss.

- Learn the art of living in the present, free from the burden of the past and the anxiety of the future.

- Acquire practical tools to help quieten the chattering mind and dissolve problems.

- Discover missing links in the practices of Meditation (*Dhyana*), Action (*Karma*), Wisdom (*Gyana*), and Devotion (*Bhakti*).

About Books by Sirshree

Sirshree's published work includes more than 150 book titles, some of which have been translated into more than 10 languages. His literature provides a profound reading on various topics of practical living and unravels the missing links in karma, wisdom, devotion, meditation, and consciousness.

His books have been published by leading publishing houses like Penguin, Hay House, Bloomsbury, Wisdom Tree, Jaico, etc. "The Source" book series, authored by Sirshree, has sold over 10 million copies. Various luminaries and celebrities like His Holiness the Dalai Lama, publishers Mr. Reid Tracy, Ms. Tami Simon and Yoga Master Dr. B. K. S. Iyengar have released Sirshree's books and lauded his work.

The Source
Attain Both, Inner Peace
and Worldly success

Awaken the Power of Faith
Discover the 7 Principles of the
Highest Power of the Universe

To order books authored by Sirshree, login to:
www.gethappythoughts.org
For further details, call: +91 9011013210

Tej Gyan Foundation – Contact details

Registered Office:
Happy Thoughts Building, Vikrant Complex, Near Tapovan Mandir, Pimpri, Pune 411017, INDIA. Contact: +91 20-27411240, +91 20-27412576

MaNaN Ashram:
Survey No. 43, Sanas Nagar, Nandoshi Gaon, Kirkatwadi Phata, Off Sinhagad Road, Taluka Haveli, Pune district - 411024, INDIA. Contact: +91 992100 8060.

WORLD PEACE PRAYER

Divine Light of Love, Bliss, and Peace is Showering;

The Golden Light of Higher Consciousness is Rising;

All negativity on Earth is Dissolving;

Everyone is in Peace and Blissfully Shining;

O God, Gratitude for Everything!

Members of Tej Gyan Foundation have been offering this impersonal mass prayer for many years. Those who are happy can offer this prayer. Those feeling low or suffering from illness can receive healing with this prayer.

If you are feeling troubled or sick, please sit to receive the healing effect of this prayer. Visualize that the divine white healing light is being showered on earth through the prayers of thousands and is also reaching you, bringing you peace and good health. You can dwell in this feeling for some time and then offer your gratitude to those offering the prayer.

A Humble Appeal

More than a million peace lovers are praying for World Peace and Global Healing every morning and evening at 9:09. This prayer is also webcast on YouTube at 9:00 pm. Please participate in this noble endeavor.

www.ingramcontent.com/pod-product-compliance
Lightning Source LLC
LaVergne TN
LVHW040142080526
838202LV00042B/2993